I0678988

Praise for *Growing Up on Route 66,* the first novel in this series:

"Lund presents an entertaining story of small town life - paperboys, the gentle aspects of life in a simpler time and the wonder of the people who make small towns the linchpin of America. Through the eyes of Mark Landon we find that the answers to the myriad questions of life and love aren't always easy to find."

--Bob Moore, *ROUTE 66 MAGAZINE* (Volume 9, Number 1; Winter 2001-02)

"If the trials of Kevin, Paul, and Winnie on the television show *The Wonder Years* remind you of your childhood, you'll enjoy this coming-of-age book. The author grew up in Rolla, and his characters, Mark Landon and Marcia Terrell, live in a small Missouri town along Route 66. The narrator tells funny stories of adolescence in the 1950s. As an adult, the narrator has a philosophical outlook. 'The road I've traveled has clearer landmarks when I look behind me than when I was moving forward.'"

--Tricia Mosser, *MISSOURI LIFE* (Volume 29, Number 6; December 2001)

Praise for *Route 66 Kids*, Lund's second novel:

"Babyboomers coming of age in a small Midwestern town on Route 66. It's a decade later but it reads like the 'Summer of '42.' An extremely heartwarming and nostalgic look at young people's angst during this age of wonder."

ROUTE 66 FEDERATION NEWS (Volume 9, Number 2; Spring, 2003)

"*Route 66 Kids*, follows the fortunes of his earlier hero and heroine of *Growing up on Route 66* , Mark Landon and Marcia Terrell, taking them through high school to the eve of Mark's departure for college at Southwest Missouri State College and Marcia's departure for . . . but you'll have to read the book to find out where Marcia is headed. . . . . No matter how often you've heard the phrase/title *You Can't Go Home Again*, Michael Lund's book convinces us that Thomas Wolfe was wrong. You can go home again, and *Route 66 Kids* takes us home wherever home was."

--William Frank, *FARMVILLE (VA) HERALD*, May 31, 2002,

Praise for *A Left-Hander on Route 66* Lund's third Novel:

"[Lund's] readers are in for a surprise if not a shock, or series of shocks. In conscious and mock imitation of the opening lines of Mark Twain's *Huck Finn* . . . Lund introduces us to another struggling teen of Fairfield, Hugh Noone--read 'no one.' . . . *A Left-hander on Route 66* is an entertaining, interesting, highly readable autobiography of a young boy . . . "

--William Frank, FARMVILLE (VA) HERALD, Sept. 17, 2003

"[*Left-hander*] is a howl with just enough of the serious to add contrast and spice."

--William Hoffman, award-winning author of Godfires, Tidewater Blood, and many more

Praise for Michael Lund's Route 66 Novels:

"I finished your [first] novel . . . and was struck by how perfectly it seemed to encircle (of course) the world of childhood and its heady veering toward adulthood. It's a loving and funny book . . . and made me recall with mingled pleasure and embarrassment all the twinges and itches and passions of adolescence. Well done, and thank you for putting it into my hands."

--Carrie Brown, author of *Lamb In Love* and *The Hatbox Baby*

"A wonderfully well-wrought [first] novel, set in a place that's still the stuff of myth, about coming of age in a simpler time when sex was giddily mysterious and life was filled with endless possibilities."

--Bernard Edelman, editor of Dear America: Letters Home from Vietnam and Centenarians: The Story of the 20th Century by the Americans Who Lived It

"In *Growing up on Route 66*, Michael Lund gives us a loving look through the telescope of memory, resurrecting forgotten feelings in the idiom of adolescence sharpened by the lens of age--and wisdom. He takes us back to a time when the road ahead was a winding one, just right for joyrides, meant to be wandered, with curious roadside attractions and shady stops along the way. Reading [his] book is like returning to a summer night when you were young, when life was full of promise, mystery, and terror, that time at twilight, before your mother called you in to wash up and go to bed, when you were playing a leisurely game of kick-the-can and wished that the game could just go on and on. Fortunately, Lund promises that it will go on, in the second book in his series, *Route 66 Kids*, and, I hope, many more to come."

--Eric Kraft, author of *The Personal History, Adventures, Experiences & Observations of Peter Leroy*

Miss Route 66

By

Michael Lund

BeachHouse Books

Chesterfield, Missouri, USA

Copyright

Copyright 2004 by Michael Lund All Rights ReservedThis novel is a work of fiction. Names, characters, places and incidents are either the product of the author's imagination or are used fictitiously. Any resemblance to actual persons living or dead or actual events is entirely coincidental.

A slightly altered version of one chapter appeared previously in the *Route 66 Federation News* under the title of "Slide Rules and Ramblers."

Graphics Credits:

Cover by Loren Robertson with the back cover photo of Michael Lund by Kirk W. Johnston.

Publication date January, 2004

ISBN 1-888725-96-6 Regular print BeachHouse Books Edition

First Printing, January, 2004

Library of Congress Cataloging-in-Publication Data

Lund, Michael, 1945-

  Miss Route 66 / by Michael Lund.

    p. cm.

  Includes bibliographical references and index.

  ISBN 1-888725-96-6 (pbk. : alk. paper) -- ISBN 1-888725-97-4 (large print pbk. (16pt. macroprintbooks) : alk. paper)

 1. United States Highway 66--Fiction. 2. Beauty contestants--Fiction. 3. Beauty contests--Fiction. 4. Young women--Fiction. 5. Missouri--Fiction. I. Title.

  PS3562.U486M57 2004

  813'.54--dc22

an Imprint of

Science & Humanities Press

PO Box 7151

Chesterfield, MO 63006-7151

(636) 394-4950

www.beachhousebooks.com

BeachHouse Books

www.beachhousebooks.com

Miss Route 66

Michael Lund

For Anne

ACKNOWLEDGMENTS

It is time--past time, in fact--to thank all the family, friends, and students who have listened to or read early versions of my stories. Their responses--sometimes praise, sometimes censure--have helped me immeasurably in the subsequent shaping of material into fiction.

I must once again specifically thank Robin Sedgwick for editorial suggestions in the preparation of this manuscript. And I wish to acknowledge my continuing gratitude to Dr. Bud Banis, my publisher, for his patience, his generosity, and his friendship.

As always, any errors in fact or inconsistencies of narration in the pages that follow are attributable solely to the author.

Miss Route 66

Michael Lund

Prologue: Belly Dance

"If I wet it, Susan," Mr. Pierce said, dipping his cigarette-browned index finger into the water of the Coke glass before him, "and then put my finger on the lip of the glass. . . ."

We were sitting in a booth at Fanny's Dairy Delite one Saturday more than twenty years ago, me a naive twelfth grader and he the worldly high school assistant principal. Me a declared contestant for the coveted crown of Miss Route 66, he a long-time promoter of that Fairfield beauty pageant.

"Yes?" I asked, wondering then what it was he was going to show me, wondering now at how innocent I must have been not to pick up on his intent from the first.

"If I circle the glass," he continued, his finger moving slowly around the rim. "If I circle the glass with just the right pressure, at just the right speed--like this--it will make a note."

And, indeed, a sound did rise up out of the glass, a ringing hollow tone I associated with the wind's moaning on a winter night in some romantic castle: "Ooooo," sang the glass.

"That's neat!" I agreed brightly, taking the straw out of my glass so I could try the same thing on my side of the booth.

As I was putting the straw on a paper napkin, Mr. Pierce reached across the booth and stopped my hand. With his fingers wrapped gently around my wrist, he leaned forward and looked intently at me. I noticed an oddly excited look in his eyes and extra saliva gathering at one corner of his mouth.

"I can put my finger on another place," he said in a husky whisper. "And you'll make the same sound: 'Ooooo.'"

He leaned closer. "You'll do a belly dance. 'Ooooo.'"

His voice dropped to a whisper. "And love it. Ooooo."

At this point I jumped up from the booth and ran out of the store, essentially terrified. I didn't understand exactly what he was talking about, but all my instincts screamed together: "Get out of here now!"

It was not the last time I had to confront Mr. Pierce and his notion of our making music together. In fact, the next time he looked into my eyes scarred my young psyche so deeply I'm only now able to talk about it. And to seal it into the past forever.

That's why I'm driving down to Fairfield several decades after the 23rd annual Miss Route 66 Pageant, determined to rectify a wrong done to me and some other girls I knew in those days. It's an anniversary celebration for the town, the sesquicentennial. But no one knows the surprise I'm planning for the mayor, the chamber of commerce, the powers that be.

I've always been a believer in consummation, you see, in things moving inevitably toward a final appropriate relationship. So if a process was initiated, then broken off, odds are, I believe, it will pick up later and continue to an end. Matters that were tilted out of kilter at one time long ago will come back level at a later date. Today is my time to set things straight in the small town of my birth.

This belief in an underlying order toward which we move is so old with me I've concluded it must have grown out of my childhood. Even the onomatopoetic sound of my name--my maiden name, that is, "Bell"--asserts, to me at least, the resonance of a perfect note, intention and fulfillment in one sound.

My family too was a harmonious whole throughout my growing up, as father, mother, older sister, and I shared a sense of destiny, the wholeness of clan. Not that we thought of ourselves as upper class, above others, but we were the Bells of Fairfield, Missouri, nuclear family in a small town at the heart of the country.

Tricia and I grew up in a close neighborhood too, several dozen parents raising a generation of young people in an area so unified we kids called it the "Circle." It was a new section on the edge of town then, frame and brick two-bedroom homes (later expanded) built to keep pace with growth during World War II and in the boom years afterward. The loop made by its three principal streets--Oak, Hill, and Limestone--gave us the sense that we were living within some benevolent realm, a circle of magic.

Even into our teenage years, my world remained connected, contained within supportive boundaries. Our high school cruising route even completed a circle: Main Street out to Business Route 66 (also called Kingshighway) past Fanny's Dairy Delite around to Sixth Street, back up to Main. We'd make that circuit ten times in the course of a Friday or Saturday night in those days, seeing the same sights but refreshing ourselves with every trip.

Life was a lovely song for me until twelfth grade, until I got caught up in the Route 66 Pageant. And something, or someone, broke the spell, ended the age of innocence. Mr. Pierce, yes. But there were also others.

That's why I'm headed back down the path of fabled Route 66 (today I-44) to Fairfield, ready to complete a set of actions begun over twenty years ago, desires abandoned in the middle of their pursuit, aspirations left to be fulfilled now.

All of this brings us back to Mr. Pierce, a man whose interest in me was, thankfully, never consummated. I didn't understand his intentions then, of course, for at least two reasons: I didn't know my own power; and I didn't understand his lack of it.

Let me explain. I hope my chief source of strength is immaterial, my heart and my character. My family and friends say it's so. But I also know a significant portion of what force I can exert in a man's world comes from my body, more specifically my belly.

You see, I have had since I entered puberty an unusually flat, attractive stomach. My breasts are modest, my rear end appealing enough, I suppose. But the way my hips are hung, my flat tummy--even after three children--moves, rocks, swivels, and

4

bumps in ways that, it turns out, men can't seem to resist.

This was something I was just beginning to learn at about the time Mr. Pierce made his indecent proposal. It came as my generation learned first the Twist and then other pelvis-oriented dances, all this at the time fashion was lowering the line where we wore our jeans and tightening the tops of our skirts. I could do, you see, a belly dance.

And Susan Bell with her alluring middle was an unconsciously seductive object of desire for someone like Mr. Pierce.

I also suspect I know now why the same man made so much of his finger and the note it could sound on a glass of water. Even my sweet husband of twenty-five years has acknowledged that a middle-aged man cannot always, shall we say, rise to the occasion. And that later encounter I had with the Route 66 Pageant official also hinted that leverage was, for him, a recurring problem.

A virgin sitting across the booth from the assistant principal at Fanny's Dairy Delite, I did not then have sufficient petting experience to know the length or duration of manhood. I remember, in fact, how startled I was when I felt Jack Greer, dancing close at a school function, press himself against my tummy. Could that be his . . . um . . . ?

I also had no idea about substitutions in the game of love. There were, so far as I knew, one male organ, one female organ, and one position for those involved. What a range of options, equipment, partners, goals my own daughters know about already in their teenage years!

Old Mr. Pierce's proposal, on the other hand (so to speak), was not for what he truly wanted. But more than digital manipulation was out of his reach (I can't seem to avoid these puns!). I could have done a belly dance for him, that is, but he wouldn't have been able to join in.

And now I'll be back in town to make a more complete response to Mr. Pierce's offer, as well as to the offers of other men I've encountered in later life. It's a story that will have a happy ending, I think, even if there are some perils and heartaches to endure before then. There are also some laughs to be had along the way, moments where I'll make some happy sounds (though not at Mr. Pierce's direction) and you can, too. So I hope you'll take the journey with me and be pleased with the results. Ooooo!

Susan Bell Thornton

St. Louis, Missouri

Volume One: Instruments.
Chapter 1

I would never have gotten involved in the Miss Route 66 Pageant in the first place, I suppose, if it hadn't been for the flute.

My best friend Sandy Johnson and I were walking home from school one early spring day when we saw it in the display window of Martin's Jewelry Store.

"Look!" I exclaimed. A velvet-lined case lay open on a glass shelf, the black and silver instrument itself divided into its three parts, each nestled in the dark recess designed for it.

"What?" said Sandy. "The rings? Watches? Earrings?" She was looking past the flute to the usual things you see in the display cases of a jewelry store.

"No, no. The flute. Look at that!"

I was dazzled. I didn't know how to play the flute, mind you, or even, at that time, how to put the pieces together into a complete musical instrument. But I'd dreamed of playing for a long time. I also saw it, in a moment of inspiration, as an alternative to Randy Alexander, the boy I was dating at the time. I could take up music and drop love.

Randy and I had gotten pretty serious in our petting, and he had been begging me to play what he called the "mouth organ." I wasn't going to do it, and I'd gotten tired of hearing about it.

"The flute, Sandy. Isn't it beautiful, even elegant!"

"Yeah, sure. But you don't play, do you?"

"Nothing but the tonette in sixth grade music class. Remember that?" It was what they called music education in those days, 75 sixth graders blowing on red bakelite instruments for one hour every other Thursday.

"Aiii! I remember. Mrs. Jeebers, 'F B-Flat F. F B-flat F.' Oh, it was terrible."

It was terrible, but even that sad effort to awaken our musical instincts had done something for me. I'd wanted to create a product of my own with that enlarged whistle, an entire song or even just a sweet melodic line. Everyone needs a way of presenting the product of her genius, I'd realized, an outgrowth of the self.

I had also thought at the time that music might help me connect more with my mother, because she'd had some musical training in her youth. She'd given up such interests when she went to work. And then, once she was married and had children, there was little time for personal pleasures.

Sixth grade music had generated a desire to express myself in a new way that, by and large, had gone unfulfilled over the next half dozen years. And now, as I approached my last year of high school, the search for a different form of Susan Bell's secret self had been reinvigorated. There was something out there (or within me), I believed, beyond the standard modes of expression I'd been taught at home, at church, and at school.

Not that I knew then what it was I wanted to say, or sing, or do. And not that I was profoundly unhappy in my current life. It was more that I suspected there was more, that there was other. Too, I felt my mother could still help me expand my horizons if we had more time for each other.

My sense of the world's and my own potential had an analog in the pear trees that were scattered about our small-town neighborhood. They showed us beautiful white blossoms in spring, hard green pellets in early summer, larger bulbs with deeper color by early August. They were always offering, that is, to transform themselves one magical fall day into the ultimate answer to our taste buds' craving. I wanted transformation myself, a richer, fuller Susan Bell growing out of the child, teenager, adolescent who'd been shaped by the conditions of my growing up.

The neighborhood I had always lived in had been superimposed on a pear orchard sometime before the war years. Dr. Masters' house, on the eastern edge of these homes, was the old farmhouse, now redone to make a residence significantly more grand than the mostly two-bedroom frame and brick houses surrounding it. The streets of Limestone and Oak reached west from that minor mansion across about twenty acres of old orchard. Eventually some fifty small lots gave room for military veterans from European and Pacific theaters to put roofs over their families' heads.

These trees were full-sized, not the dwarf varieties bred to give high yield in small spaces I have in my suburban St. Louis home now. Those old trees were substantial structures, two or more feet wide at the base, perhaps forty to fifty feet high. They produced what my Mom always called "cooking pears."

"Oh, you can eat them," she would tell Tricia, my older sister, and me. "But they're mostly grainy and sharp tasting. You won't like them."

We had to learn about that for ourselves, of course, but she was right. They were very rarely as good as the pears we could get in season in local grocery stores, juicy and sweet. Even canned pears, swimming in heavy syrup, were more palatable than the local variety.

Mrs. Baker, on Limestone Street--the other side of the Circle--was able to produce something that would be edible in winter months by putting up bushels in mason jars with a special recipe. And Colonel Springer's wife, whose property included the greatest number of trees, made pear preserves many families in the area were pleased to receive as Christmas gifts.

We kids, of course, had other uses--mostly as missiles--for the neighborhood pears, uses that evolved with the seasons. The little ones of early summer were the size of the balls you use to play jacks. We threw them at each other, painful if you were caught up close but generally harmless.

Midsummer pears, the size of tennis balls, were not to be aimed at people, but squashed against tree trunks, thrown at makeshift targets (an old garbage can lid), or lofted in simple distance contests. Fully ripe pears were generally too big and heavy for girls to throw, though the boys, playing war games, lobbed them like grenades. And in late fall rotting pears, half eaten by wasps and yellow jackets, were pitched underhand to the unwary. "Hey, Susie, catch!"

But there was always one day in the fall--oh, late September, mid-October--when, as if by magic, those sour-tasting, fibrous green pears hit a perfect, enormously satisfying ripeness. And I thought I could do the same thing myself: suddenly mature into a woman no one could have anticipated from the gawky, shy precursor they'd known for years.

I knew I wanted to be someone who could shut down the incessant love machinery of Randy Alexander and go on to something better. Not that I didn't like Randy OK, a straightforward sort of fellow locked onto a trajectory of taking over, at the appropriate time, his father's real estate business. But his raging hormones, barely held in check by fundamentalist guilt, were becoming tiring.

"Come on, Susie," he'd begged only last weekend. "A man can't go on like this." I hated, by the way, being called "Susie" or any other diminutive.

We were parked in a turnaround near the tiny Fairfield airport, a dozen miles from town. The format for such evenings had been officially followed by this Midwestern male: pick up girl and exchange greetings with parents; take in movie, with popcorn and soda, at the Uptowne; absentmindedly cruise up highway 00 north across Route 66. We'd been kissing for 45 minutes.

"OK, Randy, let's go home." I knew that wasn't what he wanted to hear.

"Oh Suze, I'm not even sure I can drive." He squirmed in the driver's seat. I squirmed at the word 'Suze.'

I have to admit, though, his argument had its appeal: the completed act wins out in my book over something begun but abandoned before the end. Still, this was sex we were talking about, not a thing girls like me were supposed to be indulging in.

"Help me finish," Randy whispered, and I heard a zipper going down. "You know," and he thrust his hips up beside the steering wheel. "You know, play the 'mouth organ.'"

"I'm going to buy it," I announced sternly to Sandy, referring to that flute in Martin's Jewelry Store window.

And I did.

2

I know we all have shocked our parents at some point in growing up. At the dinner table, on a family vacation, in the heat of some argument, we've made an announcement that challenged the identity they had so carefully constructed for us:

- "I'm going out for football," the smallest boy in his class tells his folks one early day of autumn.
- When her parents ask how her lessons went Wednesday night, beautifully coordinated Patricia explains, "Dance was good, but the car's fender is a bit mangled."
- "It means I'll be repeating English next year," admits dean's list student Tim as his Mom stares at the F on his research paper.

The second most famous day for such a revelation in my high school history is the one where I place that flute case on the dining room table and call out to my Mom in the kitchen, "Can you come here a minute?"

"What is it, honey?" she calls back, busy, as usual, fixing dinner for the four of us. My father will be home in another thirty minutes, just after five o'clock.

"Come see." I've opened the case, and the flute lies in full view.

13

"OK, OK." She comes around the corner wiping her hands on a dishtowel, her thoughts still on meat loaf, rolls, boiling potatoes. "Whose is that, Susan?" she asks, looking around the room as if the flute's owner is present but not immediately visible. She does not connect the flute in any way to me.

"It's mine."

"Oh, Susan, you don't have a flute."

You see, one idea about me had already been established in our family history: I was bright enough, attractive enough, but not talented in any particular way.

Now my older sister, Tricia, she had beauty and brains. Although away now at tiny Drury College in Springfield studying acting, she had been so popular in high school her social calendar had had to include specific blocks of time for turning down boys who wanted to go out with her. Her drama teachers thought she had ability as well as looks, a real future. This was viewed as confirmation of what our parents had decided when she was in junior high school and starred in *Our Town*.

Albert and Margaret Bell had a different conception of my place among my contemporaries: I was "sweet." Therefore I would always have friends, I would marry a "nice man," I would be someone welcome in any group. And it's true I'd risen on sweetness all the way to class president in eighth grade. But my parents' conviction was that I would never really stand out. I could not finally rise above. I should not ever blossom.

14

These two versions of their daughters were, I fully understand, arrived at honestly and openly, based on observation and evidence gathered over the nearly twenty years of our existence. When Tricia adopted an exotic bird as a pet in college, it was seen as part of her theatrical character. I would never draw attention to myself.

The Circle's children, you see, like all generations, I guess, grew up within a set of concepts created by their parents, notions appropriate to an earlier age, a sense of the world's order that was dissolving even as older people attempted to standardize it. And one of the rules that had spread throughout our parents' consciousness--and, I suppose, in even wider circles--was that natural talent would reveal itself on its own.

In this view, genius needed no particular encouragement--say, early music lessons--to be recognized. One's singing in the bathtub would be noticed by the attentive mother. Crayon drawings on construction paper at school would unveil the artist to the observant teacher. Mathematical genius would be evident when the toddler riding in a grocery cart spotted at eye level the product with the cheapest price per unit of weight on the shelves.

Now, I know I've taken a different approach with my own daughters, none of whom is likely to become a professional musician or performer. I've asserted that it might take some time for abilities to surface, some additional help to bring out latent gifts. And they've all had formal training: piano, guitar, singing, dance, sports, anything they showed the least inclination to try or even the lack of energy necessary to stop me from signing them up for lessons. It's a typical reaction, I guess, me reversing the philosophy of parents who saw no spark of the prodigy in their younger daughter.

"It's my flute, Mom. It cost $30."

"You paid for it?" my mother asks, credulity seeping into her expression. "You used your baby-sitting money to . . . to buy a flute you don't know how to play?"

My mother did know how to play. She'd had lessons for half a dozen years in grade school and high school and even considered attending a music conservatory. Her own training led her to conclude that I had no special gift. I didn't show perfect pitch singing hymns in Sunday school, nor had Mrs. Jeebers' tonette produced the obvious rich sounds and delicate phrasing of a future performer. So, me buy a flute? It made no sense.

Thirty dollars, by the way, sounds pretty cheap today for a functioning flute, but that's what I used to purchase a finely crafted musical instrument, which, as you'll learn, changed my life. It needed some minor work, I would find: pads and cork replaced, hinges cleaned and oiled, the wood polished. But it was more than adequate for the beginner I most certainly was.

Cocking her head to one side, my mother studies me and the flute. "It's yours?" she says again, less disbelieving.

"It is. Will you help me learn to play?"

Wiping her hands again, she drapes the towel over her shoulder and steps to the table. She picks up the case and smiles, a funny, whimsical smile.

"Let's go into the living room."

There she takes out the flute's three pieces: head, body, and foot. The cork is dry, but she knows there's a small container of wax somewhere in the case to soften it. The parts slide together reluctantly, but her fingers find the keys easily. Her arms rise to the side so that the flute stretches out horizontally above her shoulder.

She blows air through pursed lips, but above the mouthpiece so that it makes no sound as yet. Then she settles her bottom lip securely onto the mouthpiece and plays a simple scale. Do-re-mi-fa-sol-la-ti-do. There are some gaps and hesitations, as the keys move stiffly and the pads aren't seated cleanly on the holes.

"I can do that," I assert, reaching out for the flute.

"Wait a minute, wait a minute." She works the keys and flexes her arms before playing again: Do-re-mi-fa-sol-la-ti-do.

The minute Mom put that instrument to her lips and made music, I don't know exactly how, but I felt my life change. I had come into being as a different Susan Bell the moment that sequence of notes sounded through our little house on Oak Street, the Circle, Fairfield, Missouri, U.S.A.

It was not that I became something I had never been. Rather, some part of me so deeply buried I hadn't even quite known it was there rose up from

17

the depths, joined with the girl I'd been to make something . . . well . . . better, richer, finer. Susan Bell, future musician. And who knew what else?

Of course, it was also possible that my mother had changed, too. She handed over the flute to me, telling me to "be careful, that's a valuable piece of craftsmanship." And she stepped back into the dining room, headed through the kitchen toward the basement stairs. "I have my music," she called happily. "And my old flute!"

On this occasion, though, she didn't get through the kitchen, as, once in that room, she remembered the potatoes boiling, her rolls in the oven. But a connection had been made: the former Margaret Simpson was going to be recalled from the past with things she'd boxed up years earlier and stored in the basement.

The new/old two of us would begin flute lessons the next day. And practicing that flute, even the basic scales, revealed to me something else important right away: nobody, especially Randy Alexander, had been playing me like a musical instrument!

3

Now I'll admit, those make-out sessions I'd been having with Randy Alexander were not unpleasant for me, at least not at first. I liked kissing him, and even his hands' roaming just beyond the official limits my mother would have approved was generally exciting.

But after a while I realized Randy was kissing and sucking, squeezing and pulling, hunching and arching all to please himself, to find relief in the terrible driving of his manhood. Almost any contact with me helped him along that road. It probably never once occurred to him that I might want to travel a parallel path.

"Randy," I suggested not many days after I'd purchased my flute. "Randy, um, could you maybe stop, ah, pushing on my knee." We were in his father's car, parked again out near the Fairfield airport. And he had moved into the center of the front seat in order to drape across me.

"Pushing? Was I pushing?" He seemed surprised. But his left thigh, crossed over the right, lay on my knee. He had his right arm around my shoulder, his left hand on my right breast.

"Well, yes." I patted his knee. "Right there. It's, um, sort of shaking."

Of course, it wasn't really his knee's fault, I realize now. Those humping hips were driving it. The thigh bone's connected to the hip bone, and so forth. But, you know, it was dark in there, so I didn't realize all the connections. And what I felt was this incessant, repeated pressing on my knee, driving my leg into the corded seam of the car seat as his pelvis strained for contact.

Now, let me say again, I had sympathy for Randy's condition. His body had a cycle it wanted to go through, and I believed in finished processes. Accordingly, I had already subscribed to the full itinerary of the teenage date, which included heavy make-out as the conclusion to an evening's food and entertainment. (Tonight it had been bowling, French fries, Coke, ice cream.) So I was out there on a country road following through in the pattern that governed love for my generation.

Still, I knew I couldn't go, as we said then, "all the way" until I was legally married. But now, as Randy threw himself back toward the driver's side of the front seat, I wondered about my own parallel process of sensation in necking. Was I enjoying the full cycle of pleasure, even within the limited definition of the conservative 1950s?

And shouldn't Randy control himself just a bit better than he was right now? He was snorting, and hooting, and shifting himself around in his clothes, acting as if he might be on the verge of a seizure of some sort. If I'd been Sally Winchester, it occurred to me, he'd be a lot better behaved.

Sally was Fairfield High School's reigning Homecoming Queen (elected as a junior, mind!) and had been picked by everyone to become the next Miss Route 66. She had the ideal hourglass figure, short blonde hair turned up neatly, and a perfect smile that shined on all she met.

Sally and I got along (remember, I was "sweet"), but we were no longer close. We'd been together in school since second grade, when she had moved to Fairfield, only child of Missouri National Bank's new vice president. (He was president now and chairman of town council.) Sally had lived for a few years on a new section of Hill Street, the other side of the famous sledding run of our neighborhood. So we were close enough to play together after school and on weekends. A lot of summer days found us sharing dolls, teen magazines (before we were teenagers), and tea parties full of elaborate ritual.

But after the Winchesters moved to a bigger house on the east side of town--a structure and address appropriate to a bank president--we saw each other only at school. I later settled into the second tier of high school society, a girl Sally or one of her closer friends might take with her to a party if she wanted to avoid being picked up by a particular boy. She'd say coyly that she couldn't leave her friend Susan behind.

Boys behaved differently around Sally and that handful of other girls she associated with in our class. The guys were intimidated, I guess, by the American version of an aristocracy. Randy, I knew, would be in awe of those girls' physical beauty and their recognized abilities. Sally was nationally competitive as a baton twirler and had been the marching band's majorette since freshman year.

Randy belonged with me at the second level of popularity, though we were not quite a couple. We were not "going steady" officially, but he wasn't asking anyone else out and I had politely declined the occasional invitation from other boys.

"Randy, are you working for your father this summer?"

"My Dad?" He was puzzled and, I think, a bit embarrassed by the degree of his ardor revealed a few moments earlier. "Yeah, I guess so. You know, I go with him on appraisals, drive the car and stuff."

"Yeah. I was just wondering. I'm going to be kind of busy this summer, extra music lessons."

"Music?"

"I've started learning the flute. My Mom's teaching me."

"That's nice. The flute. You going to be in the band?"

Randy played football and basketball, though he wasn't a star in either sport. He played enough (tight end and forward) that he enjoyed it, but he also spent time on the bench fraternizing with the pep band that sat right behind the players.

I hadn't thought that far ahead, really, though, now that he mentioned it, perhaps joining the band would give me a new outlet and a chance to get to know other people.

"Probably," I said. "We'll see how much I improve, but I plan to work hard."

"You should try out for the band, though," Randy continued, more interested than I would have expected. "They go on good trips."

And here he was back at me again, his engine grinding steadily.

I wondered, then, perhaps for the first time, if Randy was the best I could do in obtaining a companion in this journey of sensations connecting to dating. I'd had offers from a number of my classmates before sliding into this more or less regular relationship with Randy. Should I begin looking again, looking higher?

And I thought too about my relationship to Sally Winchester, onetime childhood best friend.

Really, was she that much cuter than I was? I needed to study myself in the full-length mirror on Tricia's closet door again. Was she so much smarter? My grades were probably better overall, but she spoke up so eagerly in class, while I held back shyly, that teachers thought of her as bright.

Was she so much more profoundly talented? She had gone twice to the Midwest regional baton twirling competition in Kansas City and, according to her reports, failed to win a prize only because the judges favored those girls from big cities--St. Louis, Omaha, Tulsa.

Stories in the *Fairfield Daily Mirror* recounted her local successes and her outstanding performances beyond the county. And pictures of any parade included Sally in her short skirt, tasseled jacket, bright smile. So it was assumed she was a superior being, a goddess spending a last few years with us mere mortals before an apotheosis into distant stardom.

I remembered the two of us contemplating a fantasy world of princes and princesses in her backyard playhouse. Our two Barbies were dressed the same and had the same aspirations. Each was to be found by the Ken of her dreams. What had happened to advance Sally so far beyond me in the fulfillment of such hopes?

"You should get Sally Winchester to help you with the flute," said Randy out of nowhere.

"She doesn't, um, play the flute."

"Oh, I don't know. It's like a baton, though, isn't it. It's how you hold it, I bet, the fingers twirling and all."

Was it right there that my sublimated resentment of Sally Winchester slid into something closer to rivalry with her? It might have been. It might very well have been.

4

Why didn't I know more about my own potential as a musical instrument, that is, as a woman capable of experiencing pleasure? Perhaps because my mother's version of the famous "birds and the bees" talk was really a "birds and bees and pears" talk.

"I want to explain where pears . . . you know, the kind Mrs. Baker puts up . . . I want to explain where pears come from," she said one dark winter evening.

The illustration she chose was close to hand, of course, with pear trees in most of the yards of the Circle. And, well, the shape of that fruit reinforced the most important point all mothers in those days wanted daughters to remember: pear shape equals pregnancy, which you do not want.

Our mothers meant pregnancy before marriage, naturally, but there was an undercurrent in those days too of not wanting pregnancy even in marriage. Motherhood and children were desired, certainly. But pregnancy was an unavoidable nuisance.

As even the most casual observer knows, the female body's shape changes in the nine months of an embryo's development. But pride in that phase of motherhood itself was only in its infancy in the early 1960s. It would grow large, of course, in later phases of the women's liberation movement, but a Victorian desire to hide or disguise female anatomy lingered in the Midwestern small towns of mid-century.

"You know that boys and girls are different," began my mother deliberately. My father, of course, was not involved in this discussion. "It's only the girls who have babies."

Now that I think about it, our father was seldom in the house before supper time, and mother and daughters had plenty of time and space for their activities. After dinner, Dad generally watched TV and dozed, so again we were left in our female places with our feminine projects.

My father worked for the telephone company, starting out in the field but steadily moving up to the position of branch supervisor. It was all Bell and AT&T in those days, of course, a monopoly sure, but, hey!, the phones always worked. While veteran employees like my father had job security and good long-term benefits, we never considered ourselves particularly well-off.

"Girls are the flowers," my mother went on. "You bloom on the tree, white and beautiful."

My memory of this scene places it in the evening, something like 8 o'clock. We're in my parents' bedroom on the main floor (we sisters have rooms and a bath built into two thirds of the former attic). It's a strain for my mother, but I give her credit for committing herself to carry this lesson through to the end.

"You're like a flower here," she says, gesturing discreetly below her waist. "The petals are . . . well . . . sort of like your legs. And in the deepest part there, you have the . . . the beginnings of a baby."

I'm sure I must ask some questions in here, though I don't remember precisely. My inquiry and her response make vague pictures in my mind. I sketch out only an approximate scenario of events. Perhaps junior high science helps me understand eggs and fertilization, so, over time, I will be able to fill in (I won't say "flesh out"!) the gaps in my mother's account.

"And then the man comes, like the bee with his stinger," says my Mom, frowning and waving a hand, one finger extended. She knows it's not a stinger, and she will be more accurate anatomically shortly. But she's sure I should be cautious in this whole business, aware of all potential for harm.

I don't think of my own parents in this process, of course, my attractive mother, who looks young and still has her figure, and my overweight father. I know from family photographs that my father had been slim when they were first married. But he began a middle-aged spread in his mid-thirties that advanced steadily for a decade. In fact, now that I think about it, at the time I brought home my flute, my father could easily be said to have a pear-shaped body!

"A man's . . . member . . . ," offers my Mom. She's gone beyond "stinger" but she can't make herself say the word "penis." "His member goes in . . . in the flower."

While this is certainly not an attractive idea to me, it's not really frightening. Of course, the only "members" I've seen are those of male infants having their diapers changed. Sandy Johnson did, somehow, come across a science textbook from a college anatomy class, and it provided us with the curved outline of relaxed masculinity. That drawing revealed neither firmness nor size.

"And . . . and . . . once the pollen . . . the, well, the whatever, from the man . . . finds the inside of the flower, the seed sort of, it's started, the fruit."

Much of this remains academic to me, not pictured clearly, not felt as something that will someday happen to my body. I've seen no pictures of my mother's body as pear-shaped, and I don't connect my future to the women I've known who were expecting.

My mother cannot bring herself to explain what happens to male and female organs in sexual excitement or to provide any clue that the event of impregnation is not instantaneous. I don't resent her leaving these holes in her "birds and bees and pears" talk now, but later I realize that knowing all the stages would have been more satisfying to me. I do, after all, like to see things through to the end.

Right now with my mother talking, I don't even have a refined vision of my own adult body before pregnancy. I'm just entering puberty, carrying the chubbiness of my preteen years toward a slender and taller maturity. While I certainly don't have the pear shape of pregnancy, I also don't enjoy the full hips and breasts of womanhood.

"And that's where babies come from!" Mother announces with enormous pride and relief. The discussion is over. At no time did the idea that this activity might be pleasurable peek around the corners of my mother's labored (sorry!) presentation.

So, some years later, when Randy Alexander began his exploration of the land of desire, I expected nothing for myself. Oh, I'd heard from my sister Tricia and from other older girls that necking was exciting, but part of the thrill, as I understood it, was its forbidden nature. You were breaking the rules.

Movies taught me that kissing is something to make women swoon, that the embrace of two strong arms is a comfort. But the stirring in my groin and the tingling in my nipples that arose when we were parked on Lovers' Lane was puzzling. What is this, I asked, and where exactly does it go?

My parents, bless them, had given no clue to this pleasure. The peck on the cheek Mother gave Father when he went to work and when he came home each day was regular, friendly, sincere. And I know, years later, that there was genuine love throughout their years of stable union. But I never had a sign that they enjoyed physical intimacy until I was in college and dating the man I myself would marry.

Maybe it had to do with my father's getting overweight while my mother stayed slim in their forties, the time I was wondering about all this. If I let my memory actually shape an image of that twice-daily exchange of marital affection, the kiss of parting and return, it's not an encouraging picture. I see my slender mother reach up, standing on her toes. My father does not lean over but stands erect, and his protruding belly forces my mother to arch over it to reach his lips.

It's the cushy job of supervisor, in part. Dad no longer has to lug tools from the service truck and

29

climb poles to repair broken equipment or string new lines. There are no weekend or night calls he must answer. He sits at a desk now, reading reports and studying plans for improvements. His longest walk of the day is to the water cooler, the coffee machine, the meeting room. He enjoys the less strenuous workday even at the expense of jokes from his former co-workers. In time, it's almost a matter of pride to him that he's off the line and out of shape.

And, of course, his name. It turns him into a stationary target for company humor. No one working for the phone company should have our name unless, a direct descendant of Alexander Graham Bell, he owns the company.

5

I have painted Randy in a negative light so far, I know. Now I want to give him more credit.

After all, when we were parking he was naturally intent on his own goals, and it never occurred to him (nor would it have occurred to any of his fellows) that he had responsibilities to help me reach mine. In this he wasn't untypical. And in always stopping when I asked, he may even have distinguished himself from others of his sex. Although it was inadvertent, Randy also revealed to me what would give me the upper hand in many a relationship of the future.

I had decided to use our schedules in that summer before our senior year to effect a gradual drifting apart. Again, we had never officially been going steady, so there was no need for a dramatic breakup. Still, we'd fallen into a pattern of going out that would probably have continued unless one of us took action to alter that established course.

Sandy Johnson, my best friend and a neighbor in the Circle, had been trying on and off for months to get me to go out with Larry Thornton, another guy in our class.

"You know, he asked about you," she told me around the time of the junior prom. "He wondered if you were going to the dance."

"Randy's already asked me. And I don't know if I'm interested in Larry. The worm farm, you know." Larry was smart and a good athlete, but he worked afternoons and weekends on a worm farm. Unfortunately, I had allowed unpleasant associations with that operation to color my view of him.

Nightcrawlers, the local fisherman's favorite bait, were raised in large, shallow wooden boxes filled with sawdust or peat moss or a combination. People would feed, water, and watch them grow. Ultimately they were sorted and counted for sale. Larry had been handling worms since eighth grade.

"That's just a job," said Sandy. Sandy and Larry had always been friends through church. "You ought to give him a chance."

"I'm sort of dating Randy, you know, so. . . ."

"Yeah, but you're not really going with him. And maybe you need to just see what's out there."

I didn't want to go out with Larry Thornton, but I was affected by Sandy's advice in general. And, maybe, in particular, I was thinking about Larry's older brother, Paul. He was a freshman at South Central Missouri State College in town, but, because very few girls attended there (it was the state's science and engineering campus), Paul and a few others from his set still came to a lot of high school events.

Paul had dated popular Linda Reynolds in his last two years of high school, but they broke up when he stayed home to go to college and she went off to Mizzou. So he immediately became one of Fairfield

High's most sought-after dates. He was out of my reach, I suspected, but still I will have to confess to a little daydreaming about him from time to time that year.

For anything to happen with any other boy, of course, I had to find a way to phase out my regular date.

Randy had to work days that summer, so I arranged to be booked solid in baby-sitting--or at least to appear so--evenings and weekends. We each had to take some vacation trips with our families, too, and without the regular meetings provided by school, I found I could minimize contact without seeming to.

All this time, by the way, I was also practicing the flute. My mother arranged regular sessions in the morning and the afternoon, and I worked on scales and arpeggios on my own. I probably played as much as eight hours some days, if you can believe it. I'd become obsessed, driven to create music, intent on drawing out new parts of myself, finding expression for my latent talents. The first part to take a new shape was my lips.

"Embouchure"--that's the fancy word for how your lips need to purse when blowing over the mouthpiece of a flute. It directs the column of air in a steady, strong stream, sustaining and filling out any note you play.

Of course, you don't have much of an embouchure when you're learning, just as the violin beginner has no touch in dragging the bow across the strings, producing that chilling cry of the wounded cat you hear at a children's recital. Developing your embouchure takes time and practice, but, in strengthening your lips and firming certain facial muscles, it can give you a new look. And not just in the face.

Whenever Randy was kissing my ever-improving lips that summer, he didn't want to let up. I had told him nothing about my new smooch power, but the way he'd get to talking with renewed energy about my playing the mouth organ suggested he was onto this change in me.

As I've said, he was a steady boy, not destined for greatness but unlikely to go to ruin either. And my parents liked Randy. So he had the right to drop by our house on Oak Street (he lived in a relatively new area east of the high school) to invite me out for ice cream or to suggest that we sit in the lawn chairs out back under the pear tree.

Through the early weeks of that summer, before he finally took the hint (the hints, I guess), he'd use an afternoon off to show up at the Bell house. We'd chat and he'd eventually propose a date.

One day he must have knocked, but my mother and I, practicing, didn't hear him. So he probably called, politely, through the screen door of the living room, "Mrs. Bell? Susan? Hello, anyone home?"

We practiced, by the way, in the dining room, which was separated from the living room by an arched doorway. Generally, we sat side-by-side on chairs pulled away from the table, a single thin metal stand holding the music. Today, however, my mother has insisted that I stand and play as if performing. She has extended the music stand's neck up to its highest point.

Although it has nothing to do with the flute or music or the mother-daughter relationship, I have to tell you what I am wearing on this particular day: pedal pushers and a halter top.

In all the recent reevaluation of myself I've been conducting, my body has come under increased scrutiny. Especially in comparison to Sally Winchester, I want to know, do I have firm breasts, swivelly hips, long, shapely legs? To find out, I've been using the full-length mirror on the back of my sister's bedroom door. I try on certain clothes, I pose in my underwear, I even stand nude in the middle of Tricia's room.

I believe I'm not ugly because boys, after all, have asked me out. And Randy's interest in me, despite the animal element, reassures me to some degree. But I can't decide whether I'm above-average looking, in some sense pretty, by any stretch of the imagination sexy.

The first thing I've concluded is that I don't have especially large breasts. But the halter accents that area, or so I believe, making what I have seem larger than it is. However, I'm thinking this from within my body, not as an observer viewing me from a point outside myself. Randy becomes that observer.

When he doesn't hear an answer to his call at the front door, Randy steps cautiously into the living room and peers around the edge of the doorway into the dining room. And when he sees me, his jaw drops and he sucks in air.

Because my mother is pointing to the music in front of me, I am not looking directly at Randy, who appears on my left. Instead, I catch his reflection in the mirror above the breakfront to my right and look up to see him there.

I've just taken a deep breath to sustain a consistent tone and to continue smoothly through the melodic line. The tightening of my stomach muscles to propel air through that embouchure has caused my pedal pushers to drop down several inches below my navel. And with the halter top above, fully eight inches of firm, muscular tummy is exposed to an adolescent male's view. It's a tummy that's naturally flat, but playing the flute has hardened it just as it's developed my embouchure.

That tummy is exposed to my view, too, in the mirror above the breakfront. I see, in fact, myself and, on the other side of me, Randy's gaping boy's face and my erect woman's form. I am as starstruck as he is. Look at that beautiful bare midriff!

6

What models did I have to judge the quality of my erect form with its slender middle? Well, I'd seen other girls' bodies, even Sally Winchester's, in the locker room after gym class. But you can't stare in those situations, and your peers don't freeze so that you can evaluate posture, size, firmness.

This, then, was a question I began to ask myself that summer in relation to the Miss Route 66 Pageant, and one I'm still asking: where do our ideas of beauty come from? I know that one fundamental element of my definition has always included wholeness: whatever has beauty is complete in itself.

Now, I don't mean this simply in a physical sense, whole bodies or complete structures, because a person who's lost a leg can be both beautiful and heroic. I mean it more in the sense that the idea of a thing is carried through to a clear fulfillment. I'm a foe of arrested development, opposed to a compromise mentality, turned off by limited aspirations.

For that reason, by the way, my Mom never should have used the neighborhood pear trees in her birds and bees talk. It may have inspired an inappropriate narrowing in my vision of certain things.

Those pears had, as I've said, so little real value until their one moment of ripeness, that day in the fall when they stood between extended tart hardness and soft, sweet rotting. That's when they had, to me, beauty. And my mother's explanation of sex and pregnancy led me to think those early stages were to be endured only because of the adult person they eventually produced. So sessions with Randy were not expected to include pleasure, to contain beauty.

I will tell you something else: Sally Winchester (who, incidentally, was far from pear-shaped) was not complete. I didn't know what she was missing at the moment I saw myself reflected in the dining room of my own house on Oak Street in the summer before my senior year of high school. But I felt in my bones there was something not right about her. And I was, it turns out, right!

You wouldn't have seen it--none of us saw it--in her baton twirling routines performed in the front of every parade, at so many football games, in countless talent contests in Fairfield and beyond. Her moving baton was a seamless blur or a precise and regular accent to her prancing step. When she threw it spinning high above her while marching, it returned to her grip and its continued rotation like a yo-yo on a string.

Her outfit was traditional--the short skirt, the tight top, the tasseled boots--and the performance was standard. But she made no errors, and each element had more speed, height, and dexterity than anything Fairfield had ever seen.

Still, there was something missing, something wrong. I couldn't put my finger on it then. It came clear only when she was a finalist at the Miss Route 66 Pageant that next winter.

38

In those summer months of practicing the flute and estranging the boyfriend, I wasn't yet thinking that Sally had discernible flaws that could be her undoing in the Miss Route 66 competition. My more immediate object was ascertaining my own form, my own beauty. For that I used one of the few measures my contemporaries knew: the Sears catalog. (We had movie stars, of course, but in those days, they were required to keep their clothes on rather than take them off. So, what beauty was, exclusive of clothes, was less easy to determine.)

"Look at this!" Sandy said with exasperation one weeknight that summer (when Randy believed I was baby-sitting). We held the summer edition of the Sears catalog open on her bed. "Did you ever have any panties that fit like this? They look like they're painted on."

It's true--there's not a single wrinkle in any of the undergarments worn by the models we see. Yes, the women all stand stiffly, frozen like the mannequins on display in downtown stores. So I agree with Sandy that this can't be real life, where things ride up, wad, stretch and sag.

"What I want to know about is shape," I say. "Are these women all 36-24-36?" I refer, of course, to the ideal hourglass figure of our age, which I know I do not possess. Nor does Sandy.

"They say that's what Sally is," Sandy asserts. "I wish I was."

Sandy is what we called in those days "chubby." She's not really "fat" or "overweight" even, but there's always been just a bit more flesh in every part than society proposes as perfect. While she rightfully resents the automatic judgment others impose on her form, she at least enjoys the outgoing personality and cheerful disposition that's supposed to come with this body type.

"I'm too thin," I lament, thinking primarily of my breasts. "I never put on weight, and now I'm nearly five eight."

Being tall was a disadvantage in those days, as boys didn't want to go out with anyone nearly as tall as or taller than they were. And there was far less prestige attached to those girls' sports where height was an advantage. So I worried that I was growing out of all the chances I knew about to achieve happiness.

"Stand up," Sandy says. "Let me see how you look in your underwear."

I'm a little hesitant about this. While girls see each other dressing and undressing at, say, slumber parties, there's a basic shyness that controls those situations.

"Right here? Now?"

"Yes. I'll do it too."

Within minutes both of us are standing in bras and panties, looking down at the Sears catalog models, up at our images in the mirror, across at each other.

Not only are the Sears' women's undergarments all a perfect fit, their skins are without blemish, no hair is out of place, the looks on their faces show no embarrassment.

40

This must be beauty, I think. Composure, composed, composition. Everything has a place and is in its place. Each part a model length and width, the whole an ideal arrangement.

When the phone in the hall rings, the two of us who do not believe we possess beauty and have no clothes on, jump.

The telephone rests on a thin table outside Sandy's parents' room, just across the hall from us. The Johnson house resembles the Bells', as there are only three basic floor plans in our entire neighborhood. Because she's an only child, her parents didn't add a bedroom upstairs or in the basement, as many others did, to accommodate a growing family. So Sandy's room is on the main floor.

"Hello." We can hear her mother answering through the door. And then she calls, "Sandy, it's for you."

Sandy scrambles into her slacks and blouse, while I lie giggling on the bed.

In another moment, though, I have to dress in a hurry also, as Sandy calls to me: "Susan, telephone."

"Hi," I answer, a little out of breath. I am assuming that this is someone calling about baby-sitting. They would have learned from my Mom that I was here.

"Susan? Hi, this is Larry. You know, Larry Thornton."

"Oh, yes. Larry. How are you?"

I raise my eyes to Sandy, turning up a palm as a question: why is he calling me; why is he calling me here?

It takes him awhile to get to it, but he's kind of asking me over. And now my eyes narrow at Sandy. I suspect she's set me up for this, inviting me to her house and telling him to call.

"So you can come over Saturday and fill out the questionnaire?" he asks.

"Well, yes, I guess I can," I concede, frowning at Sandy.

"It will only take about ten minutes. But I'll have to show you my experiment first."

Larry's entering the science fair again, a perennial effort. He's never won first prize, but his cartography exhibit had earned honorable mention last year. He'd produced a series of maps of Fairfield based on historical records down at the courthouse.

"What's your subject this year, Larry?" I ask politely--and then wish I hadn't.

"Worms."

7

Going to Larry's wouldn't, I decided, be that hard, so long as Randy didn't find out about it. Even if he did, I could maintain it wasn't really a date. Or, better yet, I could make it another step away from Randy and toward going out with other boys. Hmm, then again, I might see Larry's older brother Paul!

It appeared at first, however, that the visit would do more to teach me about worms and dirt than alter my romantic landscape.

I suppose I should have been more tolerant of Larry's enthusiasm for earthworms, as I'd begun to be a fanatic myself about the flute. My mother at first tried to slow me down in my effort to master a complex musical instrument as quickly as possible. But I impressed her with steady application. She didn't know (or let on she knew) that I had ulterior motives in this enterprise.

Because breathing is crucial in playing any wind instrument, and because I had connected the depth and quality of my tone with powerful lips and a firm (sexy!) tummy, I was willing to endure the repetitive drills and monotonous exercises that establish the foundation for more sophisticated performance.

At first Mom would show me what to do, then leave me to practice alone so that she could return to housework. But early in the summer, she found she was enjoying playing so much herself that our practice sessions together got longer and longer. In fact, some things that happened later that year suggested that her mouth and belly were firming up as well!

My knowledge of the instrument itself also developed while I learned to play music. I had once assumed the flute was a single piece, just a pipe with holes drilled in it like a reed played in ancient times. But I learned that, in addition to the three main pieces, there are keys, rods, posts, adjustment screws, tone holes--all fitted together with microscopic precision.

Holding the flute is something one needs to practice, developing the body and the instrument into a single unit. Arm strength, stance, flexibility and power in the fingers must develop so that you can perform for any length of time. And then the mental aspect of it all must be acknowledged, a concept of the musical composition--melody, key, tempo, variation--guiding the physical operation. I had only begun, I realize now, a life's work of understanding.

At the time I stopped by Larry's house to see his science experiment, then, I should have had more respect for the similarly complex operation he was studying and the lengthy project he had completed.

"See the castings?" Larry asked, pointing at one of the six wooden trays he had stretched across saw horses in his basement. "This is what comes out of an earthworm. They contain partially digested material that enriches the soil. I measure the amount produced per cubic foot of soil per week."

"You're weighing. . . " I didn't know if the word for "waste" coming from a worm was the four-letter one a "sweet" girl like me wouldn't have used in public.

"The muscles of an earthworm are fascinating," he went on, ignoring my failure to finish. "There are circular muscles, which squeeze the body to make it longer, and another layer of longitudinal muscles, which contract the body's length."

"Uh-huh." I studied Larry while he talked. Actually, he was not bad looking, but the serious air he had about things had prevented me from checking him out in the past. I did it now with at least modest curiosity. Hmm, slim build, flat tummy, mature face. I bet his older brother is even better-looking!

"That's how they move, see. Stretching and contracting, pulling and pushing. Their burrowing through the ground lets air and water in."

"Yeah, well, I guess that's good. They're finding more food."

"It's the way their existence provides food for us that's fascinating," he corrected me. "More air and water in the soil is good for plants. So is the partially digested material they leave behind. Organic matter."

Larry pulled a big worm out of a tray, and it curled over his finger and reached for something to dig into.

"How big do those things get?"

"Most of the adults are about ten inches long, less than one-half inch in diameter. But these well-fed monsters get as big around as my middle finger and can be over a foot in length. Just what fishermen want!"

I looked at the worm, a large slimy thing. And then I looked up to Larry's face as he regarded it. Wait a minute. He's smiling. At his project, or at me?

"So, OK, what do I need to do?"

"Oh, well, that has to do with reproduction."

"Reproduction?" It had never occurred to me to wonder how adult worms make baby worms. Neighborhood lore had it that, if you cut one in two, both halves survived, making two worms. Was that what Larry was talking about?

"See, most people don't know much about worms, how they live, what they contribute to farming, how they reproduce. So one part of my exhibit will reflect public ignorance of worms, which I'm documenting through a questionnaire."

"So I'm one of the dummies who don't appreciate worms?"

"Oh, I don't know, Susan. I thought you might be an exception. Someone who does know and appreciate them."

Again, I sense a smile playing around his eyes. Is he putting me on about this whole deal?

He gives me the questionnaire, four pages, but all I have to do is, with a number 2 pencil, fill in the circle next to what I think is the correct answer. It doesn't take me long to realize I know very little about worms.

I do have to admire Larry's thoroughness in this whole endeavor, not only quantifying elements of earthworm life but providing a context for the knowledge he produces.

After I give him back the form (and it didn't take more than ten minutes), I ask some questions. I soon learn a heck of a lot more about worm sex than I ever thought I'd want to know!

Earthworms are both sexes, each having two pairs of male organs and one pair of female organs. They mate with their bodies together, facing opposite directions. A mucus is secreted, covering the rear portions of each worm with slime. Sperm travels through the slime. Ugh!--this is worse than my Mom's birds and bees and pears!

Later, a mucous ring slides forward over the worm's body, gathering several eggs and sperm along with it, and fertilization takes place inside that gunk. In two or three weeks, one or two worms hatch from a capsule formed by the mucous ring.

"The new worm starts eating its way through the ground, leaving castings," Larry concludes. "And the whole process starts again. Aren't they great?"

"What do the worms eat, anyway?"

"Anything that's in the ground. Say you're a worm living under a pear tree. You know the ones in your back yard?"

I do, of course. But I wonder how he knows about them.

"In, oh, October, November, they ripen, rot, fall to the ground."

"Yeah, the wasps and yellow jackets are all over them."

"Well, they eat some, and birds do. What's left of the pairs decays and decomposes, becomes part of Mother Earth. And through Mother Earth goes the earthworm, eating old pear stuff and leaving castings, opening the soil for air and moisture, fertilizing it so new pear trees can grow, blossom, bear fruit. It's a cycle."

He puts the worm he's been passing from hand to hand back into the tray. It scrambles (if a worm can "scramble"?) to get back underground. I look up at Larry, obviously enraptured by his project, the science of castings.

Suddenly, Larry's giant worm reminds me of Randy's "mouth organ." These boys want me to pay attention to their pet projects. I think, instead, of my flute, its clean lines and sweet tone. I recall my slender self in the mirror of my dining room, the instrument held straight out, my belly tight. Boys, I conclude--they can wait.

8

Boys can wait, but what about men?

That's what I thought when I got into the car to leave Larry Thornton's house because, walking up the sidewalk big as life, was a man--Larry's brother, Paul. And, my goodness, what a good looking man he was! Several inches taller than his brother, slender and athletic, possessing all the glamour of college.

Remember, in those days many young men finished their education with high school, going to work on the family farm, joining the military, taking up a trade. And choosing to go to South Central Missouri State College in Fairfield, where rigorous math and science departments weeded out the less able in a torturous first year, was a strong statement. Only a handful of women had ever attended, most daughters of faculty members, so it was very much a man's world.

That local campus had a significant place in the Cold War era, the time when America was designing and building the explosives and delivery systems that gave substance to a foreign policy of deterrence. At such institutions across the country budding scientists and engineers were getting the training necessary to protect our way of life.

There was, I now realize, a very phallic symbol of these American men preparing to build (or destroy, if necessary) the future: the slide rule. Before computers, even before hand-held calculators, these

49

amplified wooden rulers were holstered at the hip of nearly every SCMSC student, including Paul Thornton.

The slide rule generated approximate calculations when its thin central rod was moved left or right between two calibrated side bars and a glass frame with a hairline marker was positioned at the appropriate spot. The whole was kept in a leather case, twelve or sixteen inches long, and hooked to the owner's belt.

So this product of Fairfield High, Paul Thornton, wearing the symbol of collegiate masculinity and striding toward his front porch, existed several levels of awe above the worm farmer I'd just been talking with. And it occurred to me that I might like to have him explain rocket propulsion, target range, and product yield at some length for me.

Such an exchange wasn't going to happen today, however. For at the male hip without the slide rule came none other than my world's reigning female, Sally Winchester. No slide rule hung by her side, of course, but her two hips swung back and forth, close and far, up and down as she walked with Paul.

"Oh, hi, Susan," she sang out cheerfully. "Were you taking part in Larry's experiment?"

"I was, um, answering some of his questions." Sally lived one block over and two blocks east.

"Paul, you know Susan, don't you? Susan Bell, Tricia's little sister."

Well, thanks, Sally! Just how I want to be thought of, as an inferior, younger version.

"Sure, hi, Susan." Then he turned to Sally. "We're set for tonight? The movies?"

"I'll be ready. That will be after my workout, of course."

I assumed this meant her baton twirling workout. Sally had no summer job, no baby-sitting, no waitressing. Her life was conditioning, contests, competition.

Sally smiled her famous smile, blessing us all, and bounced on her toes. Her ample bosom bounced too, I noted, within the tight embrace of her bra and blouse. Then she spun on her heel and walked on down the sidewalk. I, baby-sitter and newly recruited worm enthusiast, had to get home.

I was driving, by the way, our family's second car, a cute little 1960 Rambler American. This automobile, my husband has informed me, was among the first well designed compact cars of the postwar years, but it came somewhat ahead of its true time. There was no gas crisis in this decade, no oil cartel, no sense of environmental danger in burning fossil fuel.

As prosperity continued through the 1960s (according to my resident automobile authority), so did the size of the middle class's second family car, leaving this reliable, functional model to expire with its parent company, American Motors (derived from Nash/Hudson). The Rambler American idea would be reborn at a later time, of course, mostly in the form of Japanese and European imports, as, in the 1970s, economy became more important than size and power.

The roads on which the efficient Rambler traveled were also changing over time, especially Route 66, the highway that inspired our annual beauty pageant. What John Steinbeck had called America's "Mother Road" was being replaced by Interstate 44, taking a new route as a four-lane divided highway north of town. (Information about this famous highway was something I had to learn in connection with the pageant, so my husband doesn't need to lecture me on this topic.) As I think about what the "Mother" Road meant from the perspective of several decades later, it occurs to me that one can't see it as particularly feminine.

The original road had come from Chicago and St. Louis into town from the northeast, run south on Fairfield's Main Street for about a mile, then turned west to head out of town toward Springfield, Joplin, Tulsa, and the great West. In driving home after seeing both of the Thornton boys, I would cross Main and travel down Kingshighway (the first, in-town rerouting of Route 66) before turning off into the area of the former pear orchard, my neighborhood, the Circle. The high school cruising route that we'd all driven hundreds of times also incorporated some of this path: the section along Main Street out to Business Route 66 past Fanny's Dairy Delite.

In some sense, then, we were all traveling within the paths of history. I couldn't see where they all led, of course, nor truly recognize how many people had been guided by the same directions in the past. Perhaps I understood the grid organizing traffic, but I certainly couldn't grasp the forces that had shaped that grid in the first place.

If the highway was a man's way, the pageant was a girl's way. We didn't aspire to build cars or race them, to survey for roads or construct them. Instead, we aspired to be things of beauty, objects of desire, the cars that are driven.

The Miss Route 66 Pageant resembled beauty contests in other communities throughout the country, calling for evening gown and swimsuit beauty; musical, artistic, or dramatic talent; qualities of congeniality, sensitivity, poise. These were the same things that determined a girl's success in other arenas, though the categories of achievement were hardly so openly admitted.

All of this encoding of values went on unrecognized by me at the time, just as Sally Winchester's one sign of vulnerability eluded notice by her peers, competition judges, and the men who hoped to be her escorts. All I knew was that I wasn't the model of choice that year, and that I didn't like it.

That night I went back to the Sears' catalog and the swimsuit and underwear models, comparing what I saw in the mirror to what was pictured on the page and what I imagined under Sally's drum majorette outfit. At first I was mightily discouraged. I certainly didn't have breasts like Sally's. But then, I realized, neither did the Sears girls.

It wasn't that bad, I concluded. All of me came together in a way that resembled the finished look of those catalog icons. I began to see it most clearly when, alone in front of the full-length mirror in my sister's room, I took off all of my clothes. Without clothes that fit imperfectly or that showed signs of wear and use, my nude body had the basic contours I saw in the models. And I had the flattest tummy!

It was something I would have to learn to use, I realized, the way Sally used her body. My stride, my stance, the motion of my hips all needed to be adjusted to draw eyes to the center that held it all together. I had to be the conductor of my own orchestra. I would do a belly dance!

Now, decades later, I know that the attempt to make my belly announce who I was represented one more step on the road to the Miss Route 66 Pageant, to my decision to become a contestant, to the fulfillment of a destiny that had been mine all along.

Here once again the flute carried me on.

9

"I think you need to schedule a performance," my mother said not long after my worm class with Larry. "It will make you perfect a few pieces. And, hey, I could play one with you!"

"Why do we need to do that?"

"Well, you should set a goal for yourself, something to work for."

"But if I just enjoy playing, here with you, why do I need to perform in front of other people?"

"You don't, of course. It's just an idea. But I think you'd be pleased to see how well you can do with someone listening. Now, I mean just friends and family. We're not going to Carnegie Hall!"

Of course, I had trouble resisting this argument: it meant once again carrying something through to completion, an idea I almost always endorsed. (I could not, of course, accept it in what Randy Alexander wanted from me.) And, as I've said, I was coming to love my instrument, what it could do, the nature of music itself.

Each time I set up the stand in our dining room, took the flute out of its case and assembled head, body and foot, then went through those routine warming-up exercises my mother insisted on, I continued to feel a new self coming into being. The "sweet" Susan Bell still existed, but latent aspects of her personality or being were also emerging as well.

I understood at some level that, in playing, I was borrowing ideas or feelings from the composers, both famous and forgotten, who had conceived the pieces I would play. Too, when I put the mouthpiece to my lips, I joined a coterie of flutists past and present, amateur and professional, who studied and performed in the same manner. They all added to the original me, or to the me who'd existed when I first saw the flute in the display window of Martin's Jewelry Store.

As my story will confirm, I think, another side of Susan Bell did exist then, unnoticed or unrecognized thus far in life. And it was emerging in those warm summer days between my junior and senior years of high school.

"OK, Mom," I told her at one point. "Let's have a recital."

"We can have it right here, put our stand in the dining room and face the living room." The wide, arched passageway between the two rooms gave people seated in the living room an open view.

"How about in September, when Tricia's home, before she goes back to Drury?" My sister was waiting tables in Springfield that summer and taking private lessons from her drama coach. It occurred to me that I'd like her to see her younger sister in a new or at least different light.

"Sure. Your father will be here, of course. Invite Sandy, Randy, a few of your friends."

Hmm, I needed to work on this. Randy and I were much less of an item, as he stayed busy at work and I evaded him at other times. Could I find a way to invite Paul Thornton? Or would that put too much pressure on me, romantic as well as musical?

I didn't play the flute all day everyday that June, July, and August, of course. It was, after all, summer, and I was a teenager. Between Memorial Day and Labor Day intense times of practice and regular baby-sitting jobs alternated with periods of idle dreaminess. During these summer downtimes, the hammock behind our house in the Circle, an old-fashioned canvas one that we'd left out in too many rainstorms, served as a favorite place of retreat for me.

To a lesser extent, my sister before me, too, had loved the hammock. Young slips of things, of course, either of us would disappear into the fold of the canvas, becoming invisible to others--say, inquiring parents--looking out from the house or across another Circle back yard.

Tricia had a second, better place where she escaped, by the way--our family bomb shelter. In the early 1950s, days of worry about possible all-out nuclear war, my father had exceeded most of his neighbors in developing a safe place for his family.

Half a century earlier, when this whole area had been a farm, there was a root cellar for the house now owned by Dr. Masters, three doors down and around the curve from us. The root cellar was in our side yard, its entrance midway in a bank that sloped up to the street. My father had done such a thorough job of enlarging and fortifying it as a bomb shelter that I wouldn't be surprised if it's still there today, intact and functional.

My parents retired to Arizona about the time I finished college, and I've not been back to the old house for over a decade now. My memories of the shelter, however, remain vivid: a large main area and a smaller storage room behind it dug into the earth and soft limestone of Piney Ridge. Dad had installed battery-powered lighting, bottled water, and a circulating, filtered ventilation system.

I was too young, I guess, to pay much attention to this project while it was in progress, but I recognize it now as one of the significant things my father completed outside his job at the phone company. After long days in the field, he must have worked hard during evenings and weekends to complete the shelter. I'm not aware of any other such project taking up his attention until my last year of high school, and his putting on weight occurred during those interim periods of inactivity.

Tricia used to hide out in our bomb shelter when her popularity threatened to overwhelm her. She'd disappear after school and on weekends for hours at a time, but we knew always where she was.

Every boy in the neighborhood wanted to be in there with her, of course, and the phrase, "going to the Bells' bomb shelter," was, for half the adolescent males in Fairfield, synonymous with making passionate love.

A neighborhood myth circulated that one of the Landon boys had actually met Tricia in the shelter, probably Charles the older one. I kind of liked Mark, the younger brother who went to Vietnam, but he was taken by Marcia Terrell in those days. Tricia has told me unequivocally that this was not a make-out site for her, but a place for quiet self-examination and recovery.

I didn't use the bomb shelter for retreat myself because it was so powerfully associated with Tricia, with the effect she had on boys. The hammock provided a comforting invisibility for me.

The hammock hung from a large pear tree near our back fence. I liked to lie in it dozing or spinning out some fantasy. The breeze might move the limbs above, imparting an occasional gentle swing, just enough to stir me from sleep. Rarely, a pear might fall to the ground with a decided thump.

In midsummer those pears were the size of tennis balls and as hard as golf balls. While some already had that familiar pear shape, others were more rounded, spherical. The elongation and broadening of the base that made the final fruit would come in the late weeks of summer.

Not many days after my Mom had set a tentative date for our concert, I was lying in our backyard hammock contemplating the nature of the universe, the shapes and forms of my world. My own body, stretched out long, lean, and comfortable under the leafy branches, gave me more satisfaction than it had at the beginning of summer. I was proud of my flat tummy.

I thought of the tire around my father's middle, his sagging belly and broadening hips. Too tired after work and dinner to take much interest in anything except the TV, he was for me background to other more exciting figures.

My mother's slender build contained much more animation, especially now that she had returned music to an important place in her life. Not only was she practicing with me, but I'd caught her playing on her own. She had dug out of cellar boxes music far too advanced for me.

My sister Tricia was also moving ahead in her life's work down in Springfield. She was gaining acting experience and skills that would, her coaches were telling her, take her far away from her small-town Midwestern beginnings. All seemed well and interesting in my gently stirring, canvas-enclosed world.

"Sure," I heard a voice say. "Sure, Sally has great boobs, but something makes me want to put my hands around Susan's waist."

10

To explain how I overheard these remarks, a brief description of the geography of the Circle is in order.

Limestone and Oak Streets branched off from a common beginning, the end of Black Street. (Black Street crossed Highway 00 on the western edge of Fairfield.) Both ran more or less east-west along the side of Piney Ridge, though not exactly in straight lines as they took parallel swings to the north halfway along their route.

After about a quarter of a mile, Limestone curved south and rejoined Oak, creating, in the minds of us kids at least, a circle of neighborhood streets. The houses on one side of Oak (ours, for instance) looked back to the houses on the south side of Limestone. And each of those back yards touched on their five neighboring backyards within the circle of homes.

Thus, I knew at once that the voices I overheard from my hammock belonged to boys who were in some back yard contiguous to the Bells'. There were low fences, shrubs, and small trees marking property lines in the middle of the Circle, but town gossip, sports scores, and information about the newest model Chevy and Ford traveled regularly from family to family over those boundaries, especially in summer months.

Who these boys were, where exactly they were, and what I should conclude from this expression of one boy's interest in my middle remained, however, to be learned. I realized immediately I wanted to know.

"Awagh!" I said loudly, giving the most voice I could to a giant yawn. I reached out one arm in an exaggerated stretch, then sat up and swung my legs out of the hammock on the side that faced our house.

Whoever had been speaking was now quiet, and I concluded that they'd been looking in my direction. I decided that a casual glance over my shoulder would not appear too staged. (I realize now that I was imitating my sister, the actress, in this little game.) And I saw movement in the bushes of Old Man Simpson's yard.

Old Man Simpson, whose house stood on a double lot behind and one lot west of ours, was a cranky sort. If he had children (or other family), I didn't know it. So the owners of the voices would probably have been boys standing in or moving across his back yard.

Half a dozen years or so earlier, Mark Landon and Billy Rhodes had put up a little neighborhood store in Old Man Simpson's garage, a freestanding building in his large side yard. He'd said they could use it to sell comic books, candy, odds and ends. But then, rather abruptly as I remember, he made them move out. I never knew why.

Billy lived across the street from Simpson, Mark on the same side up two more houses, but the associations made me think they might be the spies in question. At this time they were both going with other girls, and I had no particular interest in them.

I decided I could take more direct action. After all, I had nothing to hide here. So I stood up from the hammock and strode purposefully through the side yard up to the street. Though I was moving away from the voices, I was also moving up an incline past the entrance of our bomb shelter to a higher vantage point.

At the street I turned and surveyed the scene, casually sweeping my gaze over all the back yards but also specifically trying to pinpoint the source of the recent conversation.

There! Between Simpson's house and the McGregors', two--no three--boys were moving quickly away from me. Yes, it was Billy, Mark, and someone else I couldn't immediately recognize, though he looked familiar. Who was that?

I didn't learn who it was at that moment in part because I was drawn to a sound drifting from our dining room window, the sound of a flute playing a sweet Mozart melody. It was my mother practicing for our little concert without me.

Drawing from memory, I pictured her standing, holding the flute level, her lower lip resting comfortably on the mouthpiece. Her stomach muscles tensed as air moved from lungs through practiced embouchure to make music. She played beautifully.

I gazed across back yards toward Limestone. No boys were now visible. The large pear tree from which our hammock was hung moved slightly in the breeze, almost, to my mind, as if its branches were dancing to my mother's tune.

When my Mom paused in her playing, I hummed "Do-re-mi-fa-sol-la-ti-do."

If I looked close, I could see the miniature pears swinging from branches on the tree across the yard. Fibrous, sharp-tasting, hard as the high heel of a dress shoe, they would be impossible to eat. You couldn't even peel, slice, and cook them into a jam or jelly.

But they wouldn't stay this way forever. In another month to six weeks, the magic transformation would occur. There would be a day when anyone in the Circle could step out their kitchen door, walk across the back yard, and pull a plump, juicy fruit from any branch. You could rub it on your skirt, take a bite, and it would melt in your mouth, delicious juice running down your chin.

I thought of Randy and his hardness.

Do you know I'd never actually seen it? All of our necking had gone on in the dark, of course. And whenever he got so worked up he seemed ready to present himself, I demanded we stop and go home. But of late, my curiosity had inspired speculation. This was ironic, of course, because I had been avoiding Randy and his hardness with great energy all summer.

All I had to go on in imagining adult male genitalia were the infant versions owned by, for example, the Petersons' nine-month-old son, Jimmy, a regular baby-sitting charge. Well, there was also the textbook outline Sandy and I had inspected. But they had no clear connection to the generous handful

64

of trouble I had once or twice found thrusting around in Randy's jeans.

Girls certainly had a difficult time getting the facts about sex in those days! I'd never even seen a copy of *Playboy*, though I knew in general what would be in it: Sandy told me they showed breasts and rear ends. But *Playgirl* was still in the future, and all the Kens who went with our Barbies had no gender.

I recalled the athletic figure of Paul Thornton striding down the sidewalk. Surely he had gender! But looking at his slide rule didn't reveal that which it might have represented.

Now that I think about, Randy had never seen me without clothes either. I wondered what he concluded when he looked at the underwear models in the Sears catalog. I suppose now he imagined the other sex as consisting of simple, perfectly smooth surfaces. What bra and panties covered was more shoulder or thigh or belly. How little could he have pictured the differences between Sandy and me, me and Sally, Tricia and me.

A boy had said, "Something makes me want to put my hands around Susan's waist." What exactly did that mean? What exactly did he want? What exactly would he do once he had his fingers on my stomach?

Over time, I have come to consider the disembodied voices of the Circle's middle to be an expression of the neighborhood, of boys I grew up with but who were at that time beginning to see another Susan Bell. The words they spoke might have risen up out of a collective consciousness (Fairfield's adolescent masculinity), representing a recognition of change in me as I moved beyond "sweetness" and acknowledging my body and my identity in a new way, a rival to Sally Winchester.

Standing at the edge of the street in front of my house that summer day, I didn't quite take all the mental steps necessary to endorse this conclusion. But I knew I liked the way whoever was talking was talking about me.

This "me" departed from Randy Alexander's definition: a sweet girl he was friends with, but also a girl at whom he relentlessly pointed his mouth organ. (Poor fellow, he would have pointed it at any girl he could get a date with.) He couldn't help himself, but I was now ready to move out of his range.

In a flash of inspiration I realized the truth. I was not only ready to leave Randy behind. I was ready to be the next Miss Route 66!

Volume Two: Ensemble. Chapter 1

To enter the Miss Route 66 Pageant, girls had to meet with Mr. Pierce, Fairfield High's assistant principal and Senior Consultant (whatever that meant!) to the pageant. Early in the new school year, my senior year, I went to see him to get the application form required of all contestants.

I didn't do this at the high school, however, but in an office he was allowed to borrow six months of the year at South Central Missouri State College. The college hosted the event, and Mr. Pierce was given temporary space for his work in the basement of the central building on campus.

There was a visitors' parking lot at the south end of the campus, and one gorgeous morning in September I left the family Rambler there and started off to get the form. I was ready to put into action the new self I'd found over the summer, the flute-playing, flat-tummied, boy-attracting me.

Although she was not entering the pageant, Sandy and I had been coaching each other on how to walk, how to stand, how to move in our last year before college. We'd also reviewed our wardrobes, seeking the most flattering outfits. I looked for low-slung slacks and skirts that fit snugly on my hips. Sandy had decided her derriere was her best feature.

"All right, watch me walk up to the counter," she had said the previous weekend when we were drinking sodas at Fanny's Dairy Delite. "I'm trying to get a jiggle of rump with every step."

And, by planting each foot firmly to conclude a stride, she did impart an extra kah-thump to her walk. It showed in the action of her a-bit-larger-than-average behind. Her breasts were large too, but they didn't stand out on her body the way they would have on a more slender girl.

When she returned, I said, citing a familiar formula, "It's good. A 'backfield in motion.'" With the tight shorts she was wearing, boys would notice. "Now check me out."

I had decided that my hips had to go side to side with my walk, giving a pendulum swing, tick-tock, to my flat belly in the center. I tick-tocked to the counter for an extra napkin.

"Ooh, that's good too," said Sandy when I returned to the booth. "And it will work in the swimsuit event."

I'd explained to Sandy that I was pretty sure I'd enter the Miss Route 66 competition this year. I could play the flute at the talent show, even though I wasn't as skilled as Elizabeth Rogers on the piano or Mary Dunkin at dramatic readings. They, like Sally Winchester, were veteran contestants. She, of course, remained the favorite.

I could probably have gotten advice on movement and dress from Tricia, who was headed back this week to Drury. But I didn't want to be her "younger sister," a lesser version of the more talented

Bell daughter. And I didn't have to compete with Sandy, who could be my confidante throughout.

I was also a bit irritated with Tricia for the favor she'd asked of me: I was to take care of her African gray parrot until Christmas, as she was leaving her summer apartment for the dorms with the beginning of school. I couldn't find a way to say no, but I really didn't want the responsibility. She insisted it was just for a few months, and then a friend of hers, who was bringing a male bird back from overseas travel, would take Tricia's bird as her parrot's mate.

I couldn't believe my parents were allowing a pet bird to live upstairs in Tricia's room, but they were. And now I had regular responsibilities of feeding Juliet, cleaning her cage, and providing her company.

Tricia explained that parrots are among the oldest domesticated animals, intelligent and gregarious. Without companions of their own species, pet birds will mimic human speech, the talking parrots ("Ahoy, mate!") of pirate stories. They are monogamous, commonly mating for years if not for life. Some pets have lived as long as seven or eight decades.

While I wasn't to live with this bird for more than three months (Tricia promised!), Juliet was to have a profound effect on my life. You might even say she kept me in the Miss Route 66 Pageant after Mr. Pierce nearly drove me to quit the competition.

Of course, I knew from the beginning that this pageant was going to be a challenge. It meant taking a new version of my private self out into the public arena. This transition was underscored by the location of the contest, the SCMSC campus.

Walking along the sidewalk that day, I marveled at the clean order of the campus, its immaculate appearance. The lawns and plants here were neatly kept, perhaps because this was primarily an engineering school and it had all the equipment necessary for lawn mowing, bush trimming, sidewalk edging. Too, with only a handful of girls among several thousand students, it was believed that buildings and grounds needed only a lean, functional look with little ornamentation.

The heart of the campus was the original quadrangle, laid out for a land-grant institution of public education in a new state. (I also had to learn this history as part of the pageant preliminaries.) The Land-Grant Act of 1862 was a federal government response to public demand for new colleges to teach agriculture and manufacturing, fields deemed crucial to the industrialization and prosperity of America after the Civil War.

The SCMSC campus was constructed on a plan I still believe to be the most suitable for an educational institution, the quadrangle. Each building around the quad represents a way of thinking--science, math, humanities, the arts, etc. The open space in the middle suggests a common field in which ideas from all disciplines are shared. And the buildings facing that open area create comforting borders within which students are protected while they learn.

I realize some object to this layout as an "ivory tower," isolating professors and students from the outside world. But I prefer to see it as a complete structure, a harmonious form promoting the process of growth and fulfillment.

Against this finished backdrop that fall day, then, I hoped I was exhibiting the emerging mature identity of a young woman, perhaps that of a college coed. It wouldn't, I knew, be easy.

Mr. Pierce's pageant office was in Norwood Hall, which lay on the south side of the quad. It featured a large, jutting circular foyer, which, some of my friends said, made the building look as if it were pregnant.

Walking my new tick-tock walk, was I thinking I might run into Paul Thornton along the way to or from Norwood Hall? I'm sure I was. I don't think I would have been interested in other students, though. I could consider Paul a local boy, but young men from other places would have been too intimidating.

Randy had finally caught on that the baby-sitting and family obligations I kept citing were exaggerated, and he was no longer calling. Perhaps more importantly, he was finding that buxom Henrietta Thompson's schedule was open every time he asked.

There's something else in my romantic life I must admit here at the start of my pageant competition. Well, it's not so much romantic as physical, as involving sex. No, I wasn't sleeping with anyone. But I was giving in to the temptation of modest self-abuse more than I'd been taught was healthy. I'd discovered how easy and how satisfying this forbidden act was.

Nowadays, of course, it would be rare for any girl my age not to know what I was just learning--that such gratification is always at one's own control (I almost said "fingertips"!). But these were times of quiet but thorough repression, subtle but powerful guilt. (I'm not sure that's all bad, by the way!) Mothers and older girls kept to themselves whatever they had learned about the mysteries of lovemaking. And enjoying your own body was at best vulgar, at worst a mortal sin.

This discovery of my own potential to satisfy myself came, I must acknowledge, in part thanks again to Randy. He didn't explain it, of course, but the fact of his frustration in necking with me had left a significant impression in my mind. Sometime that summer it must have occurred to me that I might pursue more purposefully the completely physical goal he was trying to reach.

Another agent in this new (and, I'm afraid, potentially addictive habit) was Juliet, my sister's parrot.

2

The appearance of Mr. Pierce's basement office contrasted with the bright, scrubbed look of the campus outside. Down a windowless hallway, in an isolated corner, it was more like the lair of a spider or some hibernating beast. He was here from 10:00 o'clock to noon on certain Saturdays.

However, the assistant principal knew me (Fairfield High was not large) and greeted me with a pleasant smile. He sat behind a small desk, flanked by two tall file cabinets, the records, I assumed, of past pageants. He motioned to me to have a seat.

"So, you're coming out of your shell, eh, Susan? Going to step up on the stage and wow the judges."

"I . . . um, I think I will enter. But I need to find out all about the requirements, the different categories of competition, you know."

There were papers stacked loosely on Mr. Pierce's desk. The cigarette dangling from the fist of his left hand and an ashtray overflowing with butts added to a sense of disorder in the office, of things not quite put away or taken care of.

"Sure, sure," he said. "Here's our manual," he pulled a stapled package of duplicated sheets from a desk drawer. "And the application. You'll need your parents' signature, of course."

"Yes. I've talked to them." This was not true, but I didn't think they'd object once I told them. After all, their older daughter had blazed the way for a Bell girl to assume a public identity in Fairfield and beyond.

"The evening gown is straightforward. Just go down to Simpson's Clothing Store and they'll fix you up. As for swimsuits . . . hmm, what size would you be? Let me see."

He gestured for me to stand up, moving himself around the desk to get a better view. I could see that one corner of his shirt was not completely tucked in the waistband of his trousers.

I stood, a bit nervously. "I'm a . . . Junior Seven."

"Yes, I can see that. Very nice. You might, with your figure, ah, think of a two-piece suit. More of the girls go with them each year. Yes, I think so."

He seemed almost ready to reach out toward me, to confirm by touch what his eyes told him.

He stopped there by the side of his desk, though, and said pleasantly, "And what will your talent be?"

"I play the flute," I offered, sitting down again.

"All you girls will probably be trying for first runner-up, anyway," he chuckled. "Sally's so good." His eyes got hazy for a moment, imagining, I suppose, her baton whirling, her legs kicking up her skirt as she marched, that high bosom. "Still, there's always a chance . . . if . . . ." His voice trailed off, and his eyes refocused on me.

"There's an organizational meeting in two weeks. Bring your completed form. I may have to see you again, individually."

He gave me a thin smile and a bit of a wink with this last statement, though I made little of it at the time. I was happy enough to have taken this first step, to have followed through on my new sense of self. I didn't know then how far this step would take me, not just in the pageant but in my understanding of how people pursue their destinies. Nearly all the contestants who came to that organizational meeting would find their lives affected in ways they never anticipated.

I couldn't wait to tell Sandy about my progress. I would see her in school the next day, of course. But school was the place where merely "sweet" Susan Bell existed. And the environment of high school seemed limiting after my visit to the college.

Fairfield High School lay about four blocks east of downtown and the college on 10th Street. It had replaced what was invariably called "The Old High School," even though this earlier building, one block closer to town, was officially named "Fairfield Junior High School" at the time and for the next several decades.

Our beige brick, two-story building was architecturally consistent with nearly every other high school built in Middle America in the mid-1950s: entrance with principal's office and library at one end; classrooms across the main section; a combination gymnasium/auditorium with cafeteria behind at the other end.

While the population rose steadily in the 1960s, 70s, and 80s, F.H.S. survived in its basic shape. Newer elementary and middle schools provided extra space, and grades eight and nine were eventually shifted out of the high school. So when any of us returned, our past remained visible in this unchanging structure.

There was also a graduation of buildings that went along with graduating students: from the small elementary schools to larger junior high to even bigger high school and to college. I liked this sense of progression, of a process that moved from beginning to end, from small to large, from childhood to adulthood.

I hoped that I, too, like the butterfly emerging after larva and cocoon phases, was leaving behind not just buildings but states of being in my movement through these structures.

My sex life had certainly evolved, as I've said, to a new stage, though I wasn't sure I should call it progress. I had reached this latest plateau almost before I knew what I was up to.

It emerged in part from my modeling swimsuits in front of the full-length mirror in Tricia's room. I had two standard one-piece suits, one of which I (and later my mother) assumed I would wear at the pageant. But I also used bra and panties to imagine what a two-piece might do.

I practiced my walk, of course, concentrating on the side-to-side slide of my hips, measuring the ride of my flat belly. I considered my middle exposed, my middle covered.

I was watched in such displays by Tricia's parrot, who occupied a cage probably five feet high and thirty inches in diameter that hung from its own stand in the middle of the room. We'd spread an old sheet under the cage, though our new resident was not particularly messy. Juliet was, however, a large and a loud bird. She would eat any fruit, vegetable, or nut I gave her. Always ready for games or challenges, she was a demanding pet.

Tricia had showed me how to hide treats in her cage, tucking them into forks of tree branches or behind rocks in her miniaturized landscape. Juliet devised games of her own, climbing up the side of the cage, riding her swing, ringing a little bell with her thick, crooked beak.

And talk! That bird was a quick learner who had been trained, Tricia said, by her first owner, an eccentric theater manager in Tulsa, Oklahoma. "Come here," she would cry. "Pretty bird. Hello there. Pet me."

At one point, idly modeling swimsuit variations, I wondered if parrot training could be my talent. While I was progressing rapidly on the flute, I didn't know how I'd do in public. Would I panic, my hands refuse to cooperate, my breath, shallow, fail to make a tone? I looked over my shoulder to inspect my rear end. Not as full as Sandy's.

But I doubted if Juliet would do what I asked on stage, eat a biscuit, rock the swing, speak.

Perhaps I could borrow some of Larry's worms, give a talk on worm sex: "a mucous ring slides forward over the worm's body, gathering several eggs and sperm along with it, and fertilization takes place inside that gunk." No, that wouldn't work.

I stood sideways in front of the mirror. Cupping a breast in each hand, I admitted they were average at best.

Maybe a demonstration on a slide rule, if Paul would agree to instruct me. Oooh, yes, doing the numbers with the college guy!

But he was dating the pageant favorite, Sally, the baton-twirling phenomenon. I imagined her strong hands gripping the rod. (Did she, by the way, set the ends aflame?) She turns it this way and that skillfully. It travels over her head, around her waist, between her legs.

"Come here," Juliet cried. "Pretty bird. Hello there. Pet me."

It was this last injunction that led me down temptation's path. "Pet me," commanded Juliet, and I echoed her. "Pet me," I told myself. "Pet me."

And, in my underwear, I did.

3

"Are you ready to practice?" my mother called up the stairs.

I jumped (if one can *jump* from a prone position).

"Oh, um, yeah. (*Whoo!*) Just a minute. Be right down."

Well, now, *there* was an interruption, my mother breaking in on a pretty intense fantasy! She was getting ready for me to play the flute, but I had been playing myself.

Such sessions were proving that I was an instrument whom no boys had yet studied, an intricate organism capable of sweet melody. But I had to be both the player and the played.

My private pleasure would have been frowned on, of course, had anyone, including my mother, known about it. These acts were not condemned directly in those days, as no one openly used words like "masturbation." But from our earliest days we heard parents say, "Don't touch yourself there, sweetie," "Keep your hands off now," "We don't do that, honey." By the time of puberty, girls simply understood that their erogenous zones were off limits, paths to damnation.

We Bells were, I think, not more or less religious than most others in our town. A regular participant at church, Sunday school, and vacation Bible school, I absorbed the general moral code from that world.

Any deeper understanding of why such a code might have value would take many years to develop.

I don't remember my mother preaching at me. And my father was generally distant in my high school years. Still, I connected the prevailing morality with them, assuming their endorsement.

Once the flute lessons began, I did have more chances to interact with my Mom and to hear her individual opinions. But on such difficult subjects as birds and bees and pears she was, as you know, sometimes indirect, if not evasive.

My Mom obviously enjoyed our flute sessions together, though, and I was pleased that we now shared this common interest. I hadn't resented Tricia all those years when she was home, but maybe now I realized I had often been in the background of her world. In my music lessons I got my mother's full attention.

"Those are sixteenth notes there, Susan," she would say, pointing to the measure just played. "That's *one*-two-three-four, *one*-two-three-four, *one*-two-three-four."

During our months of practice I did learn some things about my mother I hadn't known, how her musical talent had been obvious at an early age, how she'd progressed steadily through her teenage years performing in church, at school, for small gatherings. But she was reaching adulthood at the end of the Great Depression, the beginning of the Second World War. There were far more jobs for bank tellers than for female musicians, especially in small towns.

I tried to imagine the romance between her and my father that would put any thoughts of a career further out of her mind. The pear-bellied father I saw every day now was not, I'm afraid, compelling as a knight in shining armor, a man on a white horse, a brilliant musical conductor.

In addition to the image of their twice-daily kiss--when he departed for work and when he returned--I have a permanent picture of him in the easy chair in front of the television. It's how I saw him many, many nights after dinner during the years of my growing up. Thank goodness he is not drinking a beer in this picture! But he is slouched before the television, his body getting broader and sagging as the chair's cushions are being compressed with the years.

I see the back of his head, the thinning hair, as I pass from the kitchen (just having finished the dishes) to do homework or practice the flute or talk on the phone with friends. I doubt if it ever occurs to me to wonder what's going on in that head as I pass through the dining room and into the hall on the way to my room.

Later events have taught me that things were going on in the mind of this middle-aged man, of course. He was engaged in a genuine confrontation with questions about where his life had gone, what his youthful dreams had been. In fact, a change was occurring in my father at the same time I was preparing myself for the Miss Route 66 Pageant. Absorbed with myself like any teenager, I just didn't see it.

A germ of the hidden man might have been visible in one anecdote of their courtship my mother had related to me more than once. It reveals the kind of enthusiasm, intensity, and appreciation of process I've always admired myself.

Even though Dad was only a telephone lineman when he met my mother, he had an interest in the engineering behind the whole industry that would help him rise in the company. And he courted the slender bank teller he had come to know with the material of his profession. She had moved here from the nearby, smaller town of St. James; he was a Fairfield native.

According to Mom, he explained telephones on one of their dates. "It's all energy," he said. "Energy throughout the whole system. The force of your breath pushes a diaphragm inside the handset." He was holding one at the time. "Here, say something."

"Oh, I hate it when someone says that. 'Say something.' I never know what to say!"

However, she does take the handset. It is connected by a long cord to another handset, not to a receiver. This young man and his date are sitting, by the way, in his car parked on the street in front of the house where she has a room. He has pulled this telephone equipment up from the back seat.

"The outside of a little box in here," he points to the speaking end of the handset. "The outside of a box full of carbon granules is compressed by the force of your breath, your energy. The closer together the granules, the better they conduct sound. The looser, the more resistance. Thus, variations in sound produced by your speech are passed down the metal wire in the middle of this cable. New kinds of energy."

"I still don't know what to say," objects my Mom. She holds the handset out at arm's length, inspecting it. "You do it."

"You're doing just fine. Go ahead and complain."

"I wasn't complaining, just offering a suggestion. Give me a script; say what to say."

He picks up the other handset. He has previously connected the two handsets by a stretch of regular telephone cable as a demonstration device. It is not patched into the larger telephone system but rather is a sophisticated version of a child's string and tin can walkie-talkie.

"Think of how anyone with a telephone can put his energy into the system, just by talking."

"Hey, where are you going?"

My father has stepped out of the car on the driver's side, carrying one handset with him. He leans back in the window.

"There's an electromagnet in the earpiece of a regular telephone--you know what an electromagnet is, don't you?"

"Yes. Wire wound around a core. More current in the wire, more magnetism."

"Yes. A regular phone is hooked to a central system. Electric current at your end, the handset-- controlled by the carbon granules compressed by your speech--activates the electromagnet in the other end, pulling a metal diaphragm to mimic your speech."

"OK. It's all a complete circuit."

"Yes. Electricity is the unifying force throughout the national system. And it connects everyone who has a phone. They all can speak into it but also receive the energy or speech of anyone else who talks."

"We used to have to crank the phone. Was that generating new energy?"

"Yes, to ring the operator in the old days. Now, keep talking and we'll see how this simpler system works."

He backs away from the car and walks down the street behind the car, still holding his handset. The cable is several dozen yards long. He crosses the sidewalk and disappears behind a tree.

Mom is puzzled. She hears his voice coming from the handset and puts it to her ear. There's a crackling sound. She thinks she can hear him walking.

"Say you'll marry me," says the voice, his face appearing suddenly at the window beside her. "Say you'll marry me."

And she does.

4

When I showed up at Simpson's Clothing Store to find out about evening gowns, I knew I would have only a brief time before I'd need to tell my parents about me and the Miss Route 66 Pageant. Fairfield was a typical small town, and word would travel as quickly from Main Street to my Dad's office or out to the Circle as my Dad's proposal had come around the car to my Mom.

Still, I figured the farther along I'd gotten with my candidacy, the harder it would be for anyone to object to it. By the end of my visit, unfortunately, I realized I would need my parents' help as well as their approval for this project.

On the day I inquired, Mary Dunkin, another contestant, was already in the store trying on a gown.

"Hi, Susan. You're entering this year?"

"I'm thinking about it. I'm pretty sure."

"That's great. You'll like it."

Simpson's, by the way, is the best clothing store in Fairfield, a favorite for those attending formal events and those to whom social standing is important. My Dad gets his business suits here, but my Mom has always shopped elsewhere for bargains.

A clerk asks if she can help me, and I explain that I am inquiring about gowns for the pageant.

"Well, you see what Mary is wearing. It's this year's required dress."

"Required?"

"Oh, yes. All the girls wear the same dress, for fairness."

"But the swimsuits are different," I note.

"Swimsuits, yes. Gowns, no."

"She's right," adds Mary. But then she raises an eyebrow to me, suggesting she might have more to say about this.

Mary Dunkin is probably the smartest girl in the competition, certainly one of Fairfield High's best students. A National Merit semifinalist, she hopes to get a scholarship to the state university in Columbia.

"So you're doing a dramatic presentation?" I ask, willing to be polite.

"Yes, Viola's speech to Olivia about the Duke's love for her."

When I look puzzled, she explains, "In Shakespeare's *Twelfth Night*."

I say "Ahh!" as if that means something to me, but it doesn't. I wasn't a big reader then and am not much better now.

Mary returns to the changing room. Seeing how the required dress fits Mary, I recognize that it will help large-busted girls. It's strapless, tight through the middle, spreading out from the waist rather than fitting trim down the legs.

Legs are Mary's best feature, something anyone who has seen her at the Fairfield Town Swimming Pool in the summer would know. Although not especially tall, she is short-waisted, and so a large portion of her sleek look is thigh and calf and ankle.

Visiting a cousin in Philadelphia several years ago, she had been introduced to synchronized swimming. She learned to float on her back, lift one leg, toes pointed, straight up to the sky. Floating face down, she could also bend suddenly at the waist and dive to the bottom. Because she was using her arms to slow her descent, her shapely legs disappeared an inch at a time.

Of course, this athletic sport was hardly known in our small Midwestern town, so, whenever Mary practiced some of these maneuvers in the town pool, she was a solo artist, not part of that team of coordinated swimmers you would see in swimming competitions back East. And here people tended to gawk at her underwater and surface acrobatics.

I remembered seeing a number of boys snickering at Mary one day last summer as she went through a series of traditional synchronized swimming moves. The guys were hanging on the splash trough at the edge of the pool as she rotated her body from face down to face up. Robbie Wann, one of the least pleasant boys I knew, reached out and did something that caused Mary to jump (if one can jump in water!) and then break off her exercise.

I assumed that he had pinched her bottom. I couldn't tell if she'd reacted to the pain of a pinch or the fact that a boy had touched her rear end.

Robbie turned around right after he pinched Mary, so his back was to her as she looked angrily around to find the perpetrator. He grinned at his comrades, winked, and then reached down into the water to the front of his own suit.

I could not see what he was doing but figured he was grabbing his crotch, making a hip thrust to underscore his boldness. His behavior disgusted me, not just because of its meanness toward Mary (and girls in general), but also because he was touching himself, an act, as I've said, my culture believed was inappropriate or worse. "What a low-class jerk!" I thought.

As this memory surfaces months later, in Simpson's Clothing Store, I blush. There's anger at Robbie in my heart still, but there's also a gnawing worry in my own mind that, with all my "swimsuit modeling" in my sister's room, I've become a low-class jerk myself.

Well, I conclude--changing the subject of my musing--this off-the-shoulder evening gown will add one more piece to Sally's standing as favorite. I'm going to need a lot from my belly and the swimsuit competition!

Mary comes out of the changing room in her own clothes, and the Simpson's clerk produces a dress for me to try on.

The Simpsons' daughter, Patti, by the way, was a cheerleader at school last year, an energetic, lively person. At least she was until the accident, what wags in town called "Cross Rhodes."

Late one night after a school dance, she and some other friends had been riding in a car driven by Billy Rhodes that got caught by a train coming through town. She'd been banged up pretty badly and never really regained her popularity with boys.

Her Dad, the storeowner, was a powerful citizen, in with the mayor and other civic leaders. A lot of kids said he couldn't stand anyone dating his daughter, at least more than once. Some even said he had it in for Hugh Noone, who was going out with Patti when she got hurt. But Hugh got in some trouble with Linda Roy and ended up, I think, in jail or something for it.

Anyway, I could see right away Mr. Simpson had a good deal supplying dresses to Miss Route 66 Pageant contestants--no competition for him. This was my first clue about the inner workings of things surrounding the competition, though I little understood then how far this network of powerful people extended. Mary did give me a hint before she left the store.

"This is going to cost even more than last year," she whispered to me as I examined myself in the three-way mirror.

"Cost?" I had assumed, I think, that there were no costs beyond the initial $20 application fee, which I'd saved from summer baby-sitting.

"Simpson makes a killing on the pageant. He can charge whatever he wants for the gowns, and we have to pay."

"How much . . . what do you think this is going to be?" My baby-sitting earnings had gone down with the start of school.

"This will be a hundred dollars," she says, lifting and dropping a piece of the dress on my hip. "There's no money in swimsuits," she adds.

I suck in my breath, realizing I'll never come up with that kind of money. I'll have to ask my parents, and I'm not sure they'll go along with spending so much on just a "sweet" girl.

Mary's choice of dramatic reading, by the way, is interesting, perhaps even an eerie forecast of what is to come for her. When Viola speaks to Olivia for the Duke in Shakespeare's play, she is disguised as Cesario, a man. Olivia becomes enraptured with Cesario/Viola, but Viola/Cesario has fallen in love with the Duke, whose spokesperson she/he was. Things get sorted out in the end, as generally happens with Shakespeare's romantic comedies, but in the meantime, what a mess!

The mixups that would occur in our little pageant that year in Fairfield were in their own way just as strange, but they were never really straightened out. At least they weren't that year. My imminent return to Fairfield, however, is intended to accomplish that long-called-for resolution.

5

The day of the duo flute performance came more swiftly than I'd anticipated. School had resumed in September, of course, so my days were busier. And, in addition to baby-sitting, I had regular bird-sitting duties.

"Come here," Juliet would say to me, especially after a day alone. "Pretty bird," she'd add, and her greens and yellows were impressive. She generally appreciated company, so I took her "Hello there" as heartfelt. When she said, "Pet me," I tried not to be led astray.

I wondered if a mate for her was truly on his way from Africa, a life partner to share the cage with. Perhaps Juliet's owner would get them a larger cage. And, if Tricia was right, Juliet had the run (flight?) of the apartment in Springfield, so the two lovers might even have a sort of freedom.

There could, then, be another generation of parrots later on, I assumed. Eggs, then what?--parrot chicks, chickadees, parakeets? I didn't know. But, now that she was a regular companion, I wanted Juliet to have a good life, to feel she'd fulfilled her destiny.

Her destiny did not include being among the guests for our recital, of course. A less exotic assembly had been invited: my parents were hosts; Sandy was best friend; my most regular customers, the Robinsons, and their twin girls (aged four) were there with our minister and his wife; Tricia was home for the weekend.

This wasn't a crowd, and they were all friendly. So the recital wouldn't be a severe test of my performance ability. Still, it was another significant step along the way to the Miss Route 66 competition.

My parents had been less surprised that I wanted to do this than they'd been that I purchased my own flute. I guess the one unanticipated act prepared them for a second. And, with less resistance than I'd expected, my Dad said he would pay for the dress and any other incidental expenses I incurred along the way.

On the day of the performance, I spent a lot of time choosing what to wear rather than practicing my pieces . I don't suppose that was good musicianship, but, new to appearing in public like this, I found the distraction calmed my nerves.

Tricia and Mom had offered to review outfits with me, but I especially wanted not to be guided by them at this point. It wasn't that I was resentful of my mother's experience or jealous of my sister's success. But I needed to make my own decisions, for better or for worse.

I had hoped Sandy might drop by to help me, but she was busy on some project and I couldn't catch up with her by phone. So it was me and a closetful of options. Whatever I wore, it had to feature my flat stomach.

Holding up a dress on its hanger, I wondered if my flute playing could really equal Sally's baton twirling or Mary's rendition of Shakespeare. I had to stay still when they had numerous moves to choose from. Sally would even have music just like me, a recorded march song or popular tune. All I could do was stand and blow.

It struck me that, dramatizing or marching in place for this beauty pageant, none of us girls could be as ambitious as boys in their endeavors. Sixteen and with a driver's license, a boy could picture himself journeying Route 66 to adventure. We could drive too, but our future travels were likely to be more restricted--trips to the grocery store, the pediatrician, the dry cleaners.

Along the stretch of old Route 66 that came through Fairfield there were many businesses--tire shops, automobile repair places, construction companies--run by men and catering to a masculine clientele. Only one establishment was run by a woman, Fanny's Dairy Delite.

Boys and men came there too, of course, as ice cream, milk shakes, sundaes, and sodas are universally popular, especially in summer months. Even during cold seasons, Fanny's stayed busy by offering sandwiches, french fries, and hot drinks. It was located a few blocks from the famous Banner Hotel, a stopping point for wealthier, out-of-state travelers on their way east or west.

Sandy and I often met at Fanny's after school rather than at one of the downtown drugstores. It was on our regular cruising route through town, a convenient place to stop. Somehow we felt freer to explore unconventional ideas in this roadside dessert shop. I think it was the place we talked most openly about sex.

"Are you nervous about your performance?" she'd asked me earlier.

"Some, I guess. But it's just going to be friends. And I need to practice playing in front of people for the pageant."

"Fanny," by the way, was a fictional character, represented in the outline of a motherly figure on the sign mounted above the door. A slightly stout, cheerful matron sporting an apron and waving a welcome, she was visible to anyone driving down Kingshighway.

"I bet you're going to wet your pants," she teased.

"Hummph. That's not going to happen!"

The Delite was run by two older women. One, Mrs. Hamilton, had been a nurse at Phipps County Hospital for years. The other, Miss Powers, had taught sixth grade in Fairfield to several generations. Running their own business had been a dream for them when they were growing up on neighboring farms south of town.

"What if you mess up? Do you keep on, or start again?"

"My mom says you keep playing. Don't let on you've played the wrong note or skipped a measure."

That is, of course, good advice. No performance is ever absolutely perfect, so carrying through to the end is important. Most people will remember the whole, not isolated parts.

"Randy coming?" asked Sandy.

"No, no. We're not seeing each other."

"Um-hum. Any eligible guys?"

"Hey, I'm not nervous, but I might be if there were guys I was interested in there."

"So there are guys you're interested in now?"

"Maybe. What about you?" I'd decided it was time to change the focus of this conversation. "Anyone watching your rump-jiggling walk?"

She chuckled. "I think I'm getting some good looks."

"What do you look at with guys?"

As I asked this question of Sandy, I wondered what I looked at myself when boy-watching. The allure of female breasts and behinds was known and acknowledged in those days. But a girl's attraction to a boy was more general, more diffuse.

"Me? I go for the big-shouldered ones."

Broad shoulders? Yes, they mattered. Square jaw? I suppose so. Trim build, above-average height, good muscles? All these things were important, but none was compelling to me.

Yet I knew which boys were attractive. I knew which boys I could fantasize about being with. What drew me on?

Mentally I scanned the male body, examined it from the front, the side, the back. Initially, it was dressed in slacks, white dress shirt, and a tie. Then that figure dissolved in my imagination and a boy in bathing trunks appeared. This one was not overly tall, a bit stout, a lot like Randy.

I discarded my old boyfriend's figure and began to watch another take shape in my mind's eye. When I saw it clearly, I blushed and told Sandy I had to go. Not only did I not say whom I had pictured, but I gave no hint that my attention had been powerfully drawn to the area of his mouth organ!

My mother had proposed we stay out of sight while Tricia welcomed and seated guests at the recital. The flutists were to stay in the kitchen, composing themselves for the performance.

I saw no reason why this wouldn't work, and during the time the doorbell was ringing and people were greeting each other I stayed quite calm leaning against the stove, imagining my fingers doing what they should be doing.

I remained calm, that is, until I stepped into the dining room, saw the faces of my assembled audience, and recognized, sitting beside Sandy, none other than the man of my dreams, Paul Thornton.

6

After the performance, which did have gaffes (but nothing major), I was so excited I'm not sure I even spoke with Paul, the college guy who'd come to my recital! Tricia had put out cookies and punch, and in the buzz of the reception I don't remember much specific conversation with anyone.

There was, I must admit, rather enthusiastic applause after my playing, and seemingly sincere congratulations. Some of it was for my mother, since no one except my father had known of her past training. But she was gracious in turning attention away from herself and over to me, the fledgling musician.

The pieces I played were pretty much standard for beginning and intermediate flutists, things like (if I remember correctly) Nelhybel's "Scherzo" and Bizet's "Entr'acte." But I played them (mostly) with precision and with, as my mother said, "a real feel" for the music. She and I played a Kohler and Moyse sonatina together and two very short pieces.

Just as encouraging to me as the praise for my musical ability was the fact that everyone seemed to accept me as a viable candidate for the Miss Route 66 crown.

"Honey," said Mrs. Robinson, "we're going to be so proud of you. Our girls will be in the audience to watch you put on the crown."

Mrs. Taylor, the minister's wife, was also encouraging. "After that contest now, Susan, you keep on playing the flute. You're a natural."

Having played the flute for some decades now, I can acknowledge being blessed with a reasonable talent. This date of my home recital figures not only as a stage in my beauty contest career but also as important in a lifetime of musical performances. The pieces my mother chose for me to play were part of a repertoire that continues to expand even now.

All that was good, of course. But what sent my blood racing was Paul Thornton's obvious interest in me. He'd come to hear me play!

Sandy had to be given the credit for snagging him and bringing him along. That must have been why I had trouble catching up with her earlier in the day. She was seeing to my love life!

When I took her aside for a minute to ask how she'd pulled this off, she tried to apologize for surprising me. "I can explain . . . ," she began.

"No, no. It's OK. I don't mind. It was great."

"But there's one thing I should tell you. . . ."

"We'll talk later," I said as Tricia tugged at my elbow. She was insisting I pose for a picture with Mom, each of us holding our instruments.

Sandy and Paul got away from the house before I could thank him properly for coming. But, flushed with my overall success, I knew I would follow up on this opportunity. Before I caught up with Paul again, though, I unexpectedly spent some time with his brother, the worm farmer.

Several days after the concert, I was hiding out in my escape hammock, indulging in some self-congratulation for my past efforts as well as fantasizing about future successes. It was another beautiful fall day, crisp enough for a heavy sweater, but warm in the sun.

Once again a nearby voice drew me out of my reverie. "Is it time to harvest these, Susan?"

I pulled my head up over the edge of the hammock and looked in the direction of the voice, which came from across our backyard fence. There I saw Larry, tossing a pear the size of a tennis ball in one hand.

"Hmm, I'm not sure. It could be." I paused. "Um, what are you up to, er, over here?"

Larry was standing in the corner of Old Man Simpson's back yard. I sat up in the hammock, swinging my feet out on that side. He rubbed the pear, sniffed it.

"I was over at Billy's. He's got some chores to do, so I thought I'd come across the street and check out the crop." Of course, there were pear trees on Billy's side of the street, so I suspected that his inspection tour was an excuse.

Now that I thought about it, he could have been the third guy in that group I'd spotted some weeks earlier. I hoped he wasn't going to start pestering me, especially now when his brother was showing interest.

"You're sure you're not stealing our worms out from under our feet? You know, they're important for growing, for the soil." I was trying to be catty, recalling things I'd learned from his science fair project.

He laughed, taking no offense. "Well, I *am* their champion. Spokesman for the underground underdog! You'd better hope that my earthworms' cousins haven't gotten into your pears. Pear worms!" He put the one he held to his mouth and started to take a bite, then stopped. "Whoo! Hard as a tree limb."

"That would have been my guess," I chuckled. "There will be a day soon, though. Couple of weeks and we'll have great ones, more than you can eat."

"Yeah. Billy says it happens that way every year. Say, I understand your flute recital was great. Paul told me."

This was nice to hear, not just the compliment, but that it was from Paul. "I'm just learning. My Mom made me look good."

"I didn't know about it, or I might have been there."

"It was mostly just family. I didn't want a big enough crowd to make me nervous."

"Are you going to study music?" He lobbed the pear he had been holding off into some bushes in Old Man Simpson's lot.

"Study . . . ?"

"You know, at college."

All the seniors at Fairfield High would take the Scholastic Aptitude Tests around this time and then

100

apply for admission to colleges. I had thought for a long time that I, like Tricia, would go to Drury, a fine little liberal arts school only 100 miles from home. But more recently, as I've said, I'd come to realize I didn't necessarily want to follow in her footsteps.

"I don't know. Where are you applying? I guess you'll go here, like your brother?"

"Maybe. But this campus is pretty much all engineering."

Now Larry held something else in one hand. I guessed he'd pulled it out of his pocket, but I hadn't seen him do it. He was inspecting it the same way he'd been checking out the pear, but it lay in his cupped palm where I couldn't see it clearly. All I could tell was that it was silver colored.

"I thought, with all your science projects, that's what you'd want. More knowledge about worm waste and its importance to agriculture."

I shouldn't have been making snide comments like this about "worm waste," but they just seemed to slip out of my mouth.

"Yes, I used to think that I would study science, worm *castings* and all." He stressed the proper word. "But I've gotten interested in other subjects, too, government, for instance."

A lot of the girls in my class would study Home Economics, if they went to college at all. A few were thinking about nursing school, but that required a significant commitment. Marriage and a family would have to be postponed.

"Well, guess I'll head back over to Billy's," Larry offered.

"Yeah, I've got to go . . . um . . . practice." I wondered if he knew I was now practicing for the Miss Route 66 Pageant.

"I found this down at Ben Franklin's," he said, turning back. "It wasn't expensive, so. . . ." He kind of shrugged. "Here."

He pitched whatever he'd been holding over the fence. The silver mass spread as it came toward me, making a ring or loop perhaps three or four inches across in the air. It wasn't a perfect circle but changed shape as it floated with bends and bumps here and there.

He'd thrown accurately, and I held a hand out and caught the silver ring neatly.

"It has flutes on it," he added, and then turned away.

It was a charm bracelet with little musical instruments attached, including, as he said, some beautiful miniature flutes.

7

Omigosh! I shouldn't be getting presents from Larry. This would give him a standing in my life I didn't want him to have. But I had been taken completely by surprise.

I called out, "Larry! No, wait. I can't . . . you shouldn't. . . ."

However, he had slipped through some bushes and kept moving, pretending, I believed, not to hear me. And I wasn't prepared to climb the fence and chase him down. This was so unfair!

Well, I'd find a way to return the bracelet, maybe just put it in the mail to him. Or I could ask Sandy to take it for me. No, I'd better not do that. I needed to handle this myself, discreetly.

Meanwhile I really should be practicing the flute and making other preparations for the upcoming competition. In fact, I had that organizational meeting to attend the following evening. I decided to put Larry and the bracelet on hold for the time being rather than take some rash action that I might later regret.

The introductory session for Miss Route 66 contestants, by the way, conducted by Mr. Pierce, impressed me quite a bit at the time. Over the years of his association with the pageant, Fairfield High's assistant principal had put together a succinct one-hour presentation, carefully polished from start to finish. It had beginning, middle, and end; and the whole did what it was supposed to. (From where I stand now, of course, I can see all sorts of red flags in that artful composition, signals of ulterior motives I didn't have the experience then to interpret.)

"Remember, girls," said Mr. Pierce early in the session. "You have to play to the judges on pageant night, not just put yourself out there on the stage and hope for the best. Every judge is a potential admirer, and you have to figure out what appeals to him."

All the judges were male, by the way: Mr. Rodd, town mayor; the president of Thompson and Pollman Insurance, Mr. Pollman; and Mr. Systrunk, head of Fairfield's most prestigious law firm. The pageant emcee was a local celebrity, country-and-western singer, Blind Bill Martin.

Mr. Pierce went on. "This one, *hgrph*, for instance." He was sketching a hypothetical judge for us, inserting a little cough into his delivery to elevate his lecture style. "This one, *hgrph*, is only interested in the bows you take, the sweep of your arm, the bend of your neck. Another wants you to walk in a certain way, *hgrph*, with a bounce and an assertiveness. Yet a third watches how your strapless evening gown rides below your shoulders. It shouldn't slip or sag. *Hgrph*."

We were in a small basement auditorium of Norwood Hall. Mr. Pierce, whose main function was to marshall the contestants through the three kinds of competition, stood at a lectern before our semicircular rings of tiered seats. There were three blackboard panels behind him.

104

"Also, there are more titles than *the* Miss Route 66 to be won here. So judges aren't your only audience."

As he continued, Mr. Pierce tapped his palm with the side of a wooden pointer. It telescoped from about ten inches in length to over three feet.

"There are, of course, first and second runner-up, very important positions." He tapped his pointer beside these terms on the board to his left. "If, for any reason, the winner, *hgrph*, cannot serve during the next year, why, one of these girls will have to take her place."

Was it my imagination, or did he look at Sally Winchester and smile when he said the word "winner"? She certainly flashed her famous smile at him as he spoke.

"Mr. Pierce?" asked Elizabeth Rogers, who stood a good chance of winning the talent competition. She'd been playing piano since the age of five and had a flair for performance. She was younger than most of the girls, but this was her third year in the contest. "What about shoes? Are we required to wear heels?"

Liz was tall, nearly five feet ten. And she knew standing out in a row of shorter girls was sometimes to her disadvantage.

"There are no restrictions on shoes this year," Mr. Pierce said. "But I should say, Liz, that the right shoes can do a lot in the swimsuit. They give, *hgrph*, your legs the right shape."

I knew I wasn't going to win with my legs, but I was getting tips in general that would help me. I needed to build the whole package here, the complete contestant: talent, beauty, poise.

While Liz and I were not in the same class at school, we'd taken two years of Latin together and I liked her. If I hadn't had my Mom to help me with the flute, I probably would have asked her help with my playing, since she had such musical know-how.

But music wasn't her only talent: she was Fairfield's first really gifted cross country runner among the girls. Now, I don't mean she was going to be best in the state, as we were a small school. But she'd won district and regionals two years in a row and competed in the state championships.

She had the look of a distance runner, all arms and lanky legs. Her stride seemed awkward, like a colt's, but she covered the ground. And she never tired. There had been, however, one embarrassing moment in her racing career. At the finish of a race, Liz's left boob flopped out of her outfit.

Fortunately, this occurred at a small event, conference competition with a team from Licking. So no one in Fairfield, except members of the track and field team, saw it.

These were the days before tight-fitting running clothes came along, those form-hugging special fabrics and elaborately engineered support structures. And girls, who were not taken very seriously as athletes, just wore what we called "gym clothes" to their meets rather than racing gear. So, when, in an extra effort to extend her winning margin at that memorable race, Liz threw forward an arm in crossing the finish line, out came a breast.

106

Of course, she poked it back in her bra immediately, and refused to acknowledge that this awkward event had ever happened. If it had happened to me, I would have been so mortified I could never even have dressed out for gym again! But Liz was tough. For the pageant, she would look her best in the long evening gown.

Mr. Pierce went on. "There are also prizes for three additional contestants: Most Congenial, Most Dedicated, and the Roadside Attraction." Again he tapped with his pointer, this time the board to his right. "And these three titles are chosen by you, by all the competitors."

Oh, don't make me Miss Congenial, I thought. Too much like being sweet.

I shifted in my seat. My candidacy, my new self, was now completely out in the open, something I couldn't take back even if I dropped out of the pageant. I had joined a coterie of girls who saw themselves as beauties, as women men wanted to see.

Except for the Roadside Attraction, there was nothing that made this beauty pageant different from others across the country. Route 66 figured in the title, but there was no overall theme of transportation or the American Dream or new frontiers. I suspect the original organizers just threw in this particular feature to justify connecting the pageant to the Mother Road.

The Roadside Attraction was supposed to be the candidate who didn't win the title or a runner-up spot, someone who wasn't the most congenial or most dedicated, but a girl who consistently made the event interesting along the way.

"She's funny," said Mr. Pierce. "She makes us laugh and keeps the right tone throughout. She's clever, saying the right thing to cheer up a disappointed competitor or encourage a girl who has lost her enthusiasm. She's the spirit of the pageant."

And with that he moved into his finish. "So, not all of you can be first or second runner-up. Only one girl can be Miss Route 66." He tapped the board behind him, where the title appeared in an elegant script. "But everyone should come away from this contest a winner. *Hgrph.* And that's what I'm here to help you with, to be a winner."

Mr. Pierce smiled as his gaze swept across our attentive young faces. It gives me a shudder now to remember that gaze and how I learned what it really meant less than a week later at Fanny's Dairy Delite.

8

Well, you already know what Mr. Pierce said at Fanny's, about my doing the belly dance under his direction. And how I ran out of there in a panic, not exactly sure what he was talking about, but pretty darn sure I wanted no part of it.

Up until he'd starting making his glass sing, he'd done nothing but give me reasonable advice: about what to wear when playing the flute; about how to do my hair with the evening gown; about making sure I turned this way and that in the swimsuit competition. (Hmm. Now that I think about it, some of this was clearly leading up to glass playing.)

Then all of a sudden, it seemed to me, he was leaning across the booth and extra saliva was forming in the corner of his mouth. And I was heading for the door.

Outside I kept moving, intent on jumping into the Rambler and putting significant distance between me and Mr. Pierce. Stuffing my hands into my jacket pockets with a kind of shudder, I felt the charm bracelet Larry had given me, with its tiny musical instruments. I had been carrying it with me in hopes that the perfect opportunity to return it would arrive by chance.

Memory of Larry the worm farmer didn't drive the picture of Mr. Pierce out of my mind immediately, but it did give me my first words to express how I felt about the assistant principal: "Worm waste!"

I know, I should have said "castings." Still, you get the idea.

Returning the charm bracelet, I realized, was now the lesser of my current challenges. Yes, I didn't want Larry believing he and I were close enough to exchange presents. But the relationship of the new me to the whole rest of the world was threatened if I couldn't go through with the Miss Route 66 Pageant. So Mr. Pierce was the more serious obstacle in the path of my true destiny.

Away from Fanny's Dairy Delite down our favorite in-town cruising route, I came back home to the Circle. There I asked myself what I should do about the assistant principal and his odd talk. Of course, it's easy now to see what I should have done: reported him to my parents, to the School Board, to the authorities.

But these were different days, remember, when so much was left unspoken, unseen, under wraps. A policy that told us "If you can't say something nice, don't say anything at tall" made it easy for un-nice things to stay concealed. And that made it hard for young people to know what to look out for, what to suspect, what to recognize as a threat.

I hadn't, it turns out, been the only one to be approached by Mr. Pierce. At the end of the organizational meeting, he had made an appointment with each of the four girls new to the pageant. And I eventually learned--too late to spare myself, or any of us--that he made similar magic fingers proposals to every one of them.

Still, Mr. Pierce had really only suggested doing something odd together, not literally proposed having sex. He talked about generating notes ("Oooo!") while doing a belly dance. And innocent me, I wasn't completely sure what he meant. (That was the advantage of good old Randy and his mouth organ: you knew what he wanted!) What *could* I tell my parents?

In the privacy of Tricia's bedroom, I did seek advice from a world traveler, Juliet the parrot. "Hello there," she said.

"I have a problem," I offered. "Mr. Pierce acted really weird at the Dairy Delite today. I'm not sure I like being around him."

"Come here," she said. So I came over to her cage, and she hooked her beak over my little finger.

"Thanks for the handshake--or beakshake."

"Pretty bird."

"Yes," I mused. "Pretty bird. I think Mr. Pierce thinks I'm pretty. Or something."

"Hello there."

Apparently this wasn't going to be where I found the answer to life's many problems. I gave Juliet a dry piece of melon. Let's face it, I thought, the easiest person to talk with about this was going to be my best friend. I called up Sandy.

"Sandy," I said, "what do you know about Mr. Pierce?"

"Not much," she replied. "I don't particularly like him, but, then, I've never met a principal I like." She laughed.

"Yeah? Is there something specific about him? Is he married?"

"Sure, married, got two kids, boys I think. No, there's nothing specific, though. . . ."

"What?"

"Oh, I don't know. He seems, sometimes, to look at girls in a funny way. And Mary said something about him once."

"Mary Dunkin? What?"

"Yeah. She said only Sally Winchester could handle him."

"What did she mean by that?"

"I don't know. Just that most girls are a bit afraid of him. I know he intimidates me!"

Well, I was intimidated now. So, after more general girl talk with Sandy, I decided to go back to the lesser problem, return of the charm bracelet. Since Sandy and Larry were old friends, I didn't share my thoughts about this with her.

Yes, I was uneasy putting the incident at Fanny's on the back burner, but I guess I wasn't really ready to confront everything it was telling me--about Mr. Pierce, and even about myself.

That's, of course, the way it is with adolescence: one crisis blends into another. You worry and struggle and agonize--about your looks, your behavior, your relationship to your peers--and never feel you're making progress with anything.

In the end, it turns out you have gradually come to terms with many areas of concern. Or at least this is so for most of us. For those who finally find themselves in adulthood, the journey they've traveled seems magical. Where exactly was the victory? When did we crest the mountain and start on the downhill path? How did each of those old problems get resolved anyway?

I can say this, of course, in the kitchen of my suburban home some twenty years after the events in question. I consider myself fortunate to have survived childhood's dilemmas with as little damage to my sense of self as I have endured. And I know full well that others, many others, have not been as lucky as I. Despite the casualties in the eternal drama of growing up, however, there are a great number of survivors. And I take heart in that general pattern of resolution.

So anyway, I felt I had to tackle at least one of my problems in this early stage of the Miss Route 66 Pageant, in this period of my emergence as someone more than "sweet." How could I relieve myself of a charm bracelet?

First of all, I didn't want to pursue Larry in order to return his gift. That would make it look like I was interested in him. I needed to just bump into him somewhere and then casually say, oh, I don't know-- say maybe that I couldn't wear this bracelet because I was having some sort of allergic reaction.

Hmm, could I possibly get in touch with Paul, the older brother, and have him give the bracelet to Larry? Paul had been at my concert, after all, and I still hadn't thanked him properly. What I needed was the appropriate occasion when we might get together briefly--for a chat, for a chance for me to say again how nice it was that he'd come to the recital (I wouldn't even call it "mine" as both my Mom and I had played), for a moment when I might ask him a slight favor.

This was, of course, so thoughtless an idea where Larry was concerned that I'm ashamed to admit now I ever entertained it.

As I contemplated my emerging solution then, I found myself once again in front of the full-length mirror in Tricia's room. And now you may also see another reason I was so upset by what Mr. Pierce said. He'd put a wet finger on his Coke glass, remember, and pulled it along the edge to create a sound--"Ooooo." He was playing the glass like a musical instrument, proposing to play me in the same way. But I'd already been playing myself more than I wanted to admit. "Pet me," Juliet had said. And I did. Guiltily.

9

I worried that my sins of self-abuse might be discovered. And I fretted that every day Larry's charm bracelet remained in my possession would give him reason to think a relationship was developing. The two concerns overlapped each other and intermingled, of course, and I found myself sliding away from talking to Larry (via Paul) to confronting once again the difficulty posed by Mr. Pierce.

I had begun to admit that, if I wanted to be more than sweet, I was going to have to take the initiative, to do something. But I thought I might need some help. Whenever a young person like me considers questioning the authority of an established social figure, she will generally seek the support of another authority. In this case, it had to be my father.

Now, I know my mother was an authority in my life. And I'd gotten closer to her over the last six months as we practiced and then performed together. But, despite her domestic competence and musical ability, Mom was still a woman. And wives and mothers simply did not have the status in the larger world I felt I needed in such a case. Besides, I didn't think I could explain what had occurred in terms of birds and bees and pears.

So, after fretting and stewing to myself about the competition and Mr. Pierce for several days, I sought out my father. I'd hoped I could explain my general uncomfortableness in the presence of the assistant principal without narrating in detail the incident at Fanny's Dairy Delite.

It seemed that I'd come up with a reasonable scheme. Of course, I was ignoring two key facts of the times: a father's reluctance to acknowledge sex in the life of his daughter; and a man's preoccupation with his own affairs.

The next Sunday afternoon I found my Dad in, of all places, Tricia's favorite retreat, the old bomb shelter. I'd looked for him all over the house. Finally checking the back yard, I noted the door to the bomb shelter had been left open. He was standing in the main room with his hands on his hips, surveying.

"Dad. What are you doing out here?"

He chuckled. "Oh, hi. I'm not sure. Looking around, I guess." He turned slowly, observing the bunk beds (that would sleep four), the surplus World War II canned rations and the bottled water on shelves (supposed to last six weeks), the miniaturized recreational area (where we could have indulged in cards, Monopoly, books).

"It's always the same," I noted, looking at the room myself. "Tricia's the only who comes out here."

"Yes, it's been a few years since I've even stepped inside. Pretty elaborate, though, don't you think?"

"Yeah." I hadn't ever really thought about it. Nuclear destruction had never been a powerful idea for me. All the world I knew kept humming along in its regular way. Even when I saw the movie *On the Beach*, I couldn't make myself connect its sequence of

116

doomsday events to the life I saw continuing all around me.

"Gosh, I worked a lot of weekends and evenings to get this set up!" exclaimed my father.

He opened a deep drawer in a set of storage cabinets. Inside were a few small wooden barbells, a jump rope, and an exercise mat. The idea, I guessed, was that we'd need something to keep us in shape if we were trapped in here for weeks or even months.

"Say, Dad, thanks for agreeing to pay for my dress. You know, the pageant."

"Ah, yes. Well, we spent plenty on your sister, so it's only fair you have your day. Did you know I designed an air filtering system for this shelter and installed it?" He gazed up at a vent in the back wall.

"Yes. Um, my having my day, it reminds me, the Pageant is, uh . . . well, there can be some stress, some little problems."

"We have a chemical toilet back there," he gestured toward the smaller room carved into the bank in our side yard. Oak Street ran along the side of Piney Ridge, which created a northern border for the Circle. The bank in our side yard was part of the larger slope of Piney Ridge. When I was in college, development expanded up the ridge and down the other side.

"A toilet. Yes. How long could we have stayed out here? A month?"

"Several months, the time I figured radioactivity would be too high to venture out. But we could have lived here for longer, if things outside weren't safe."

"Weren't safe?"

He sighed. "Well, in those days we worried that society would come apart after the atomic bombs were dropped. There'd be anarchy outside. So we'd have to hide in here, venturing out only to replenish supplies."

"We'd be fighting our neighbors?"

"We might. We were thinking it would be the end of the world as we know it. And even good men might go bad in those circumstances."

"It would be no holds barred? Every man for himself?"

"That's right." He took the jump rope out of the storage drawer and absentmindedly inspected it.

"Would girls, would women have been especially, um, in danger?"

"We'd all be in danger, hon'. People who are starving or sick, they'll do what it takes to survive."

"I mean, you know, women might be attacked. Men could, well, turn into attackers."

I meant, of course, to use the term "rape" here, but that was a four-letter word in our day. Too shocking for me to say, too shocking for Dad to hear. I was having genuine trouble getting to the topic I had on my mind.

"I would have protected you," he said simply.

Dad now shook the jump rope out, draping it down at his feet as if he were actually going to jump.

118

"Dad, what should a girl do . . . a girl who thinks someone, a man, is not really under control. He might try to . . . do something with her?"

"You know, I used to get this out to unwind after working on the shelter. I'd get so keyed up, planning and revising and arranging, that I'd need to relax."

"Um-hm."

"And I used to jump rope regularly, back in high school."

Unbelievably, my father had been a fairly talented boxer years ago. He'd competed as an amateur welterweight for a couple of years after high school. Looking at the overweight, aging man before me now made that part of his life hard to imagine.

"But, Dad, I'm thinking about the Miss Route 66 thing, the judges and all. Do you think any of them ever get out of line with the girls? You know, flirting with them or something?"

"What? Oh, no. You're talking about the mayor and Abe Pollman, that lawyer, Systrunk. They're all pillars of the community. And Bill Martin, he's blind, after all."

"Yeah, well. . . . But suppose one did try to get one of the contestants off by herself, to ask her to . . . to do things."

He stared at me. Either he didn't comprehend what I was saying in general, or he couldn't connect such imagined events to his daughter.

"You know what I would have hated most about living in the bomb shelter?"

119

"Huh?"

"No telephones." He waved me back a few paces, making room to swing the jump rope.

"No phones," I repeated.

He began jumping half-speed, that is, with a little hop in between each time the rope passed beneath his feet. I could tell he'd done this a lot, as the rope whizzed around smoothly and slapped sharply beneath his feet. But his overweight body wasn't under control. The middle of his pear stretched out at the top and bottom of each jump.

"The system would . . . be blown to . . . smithereens," he said, huffing after every third word. "And we'd all . . . be together . . . inside. No one . . . to call."

10

Well, so much for parental rescue. After my heart-to-heart with Dad in the bomb shelter, I decided I would pretty much have to figure this one out by myself. The first rule I adopted was never to let myself be alone with Mr. Pierce again, a rule I was able to follow on all but one unfortunate occasion.

In general, it wasn't hard to stay in the company of the other girls, as the next events in pageant preparation, rehearsals, required attendance by all contestants. We each had to learn where we'd stand in the talent competition, how we'd process wearing evening gowns and swimsuits, and what was involved in the lineup of the three finalists. We had two run-throughs on successive Saturday afternoons leading up to the big Friday-night event.

Although I remained nervous about the competition and apprehensive about Mr. Pierce, I was calmed each time I walked from the visitors' parking lot by the beauty of the college campus. Even as winter approached, the grounds were meticulously kept. Bushes and trees had been appropriately pruned, fallen leaves had been swept up and taken away, trash had been neatly deposited in the appropriate receptacles.

And fall weather! The air is clear, the temperature moderate. It's not the dead of winter, with no life. You feel a year's end is coming, but the sure turn of the cycle reminds you that the sister season of spring will come in its time.

It all made me look beyond the pageant and my last year of high school with considerable optimism. This was the kind of world I would eventually be moving into.

The auditorium made up the north end of South Central Missouri State College's simple but attractive quadrangle and thus backed up on Business Route 66. Pageant sponsors made use of this fact in advertising the event, using slogans like "See Miss Route 66 crowned on Route 66" and calling it "America's Main Street Beauty Contest." A related idea, of course, was that winning this title propelled you on to our country's highest standing, as you were linked to the Mother Road as a kind of royalty.

While one winner, Cathy Williams, did go on to a brief career in Hollywood (before giving up glamour for the traditional role of homemaker), most girls' lives faded back into the ordinary world after a brief comet's flash across the sky. The Miss Route 66 Pageant was, I now understand, a final event in a girl's life, not an initial one for a woman. There were few places a beauty contest winner could market her polished skills, except, of course, in catching a husband, who then might take her down Route 66 as an attractive prize along the way of his journey.

Still, at the time, I tried to believe that I was destined for special glory. I even viewed my neighborhood's annual ripening of the pears as confirmation. I realized that the Circle's one fine day of harvest had arrived as I headed out the door toward the Rambler on the day of the final rehearsal.

122

Wrapped in my winter jacket for the first time this year, I chanced to look up at tree and sky. When I focused for a second on a single fruit, I recognized the look of ripeness. I pulled down a low branch, felt a pear loosen easily at the stem. Rubbing it on my sleeve, I took a bite. Ah, its day had come. Wouldn't mine be arriving soon also?

Later, on the walk from the parked Rambler toward the auditorium at the end of the quad, I wondered if, by chance, I'd run into Paul Thornton. There were no classes in session, but I did pass by the student union and the library. He could be at either of those places, or even sitting on a bench beside the very sidewalk I stood on!

You might well be thinking I wouldn't have had to worry about a chance meeting with Paul if I'd just called him up and offered to meet. But these were the days when boys called girls, not the other way around. In fact, the whole sequence of courtship was determined by the guy's action and the girl's acquiescence. The rules held even more surely when the boy was significantly older--say, in college--than the girl--who might still be in high school.

I suspect there was even more to my reluctance to break this social code: Sally Winchester.

I assumed she and Paul were sort of a couple. That was the word around town, that he'd been snatched away from all other girls by the probable next Miss Route 66.

True, he'd come to my concert. But he hadn't asked me if he should come or talked to me since. So I felt like I was standing in no man's land here.

Sally, on the other hand, seemed very certain of where she was standing in those rehearsals. Mr. Pierce had her act the part of the winner in a mock run-through of the final announcement. And she was relentlessly helpful to us newbies who had to be told about each phase of the process:

- "You'll want to avoid exertion as you prepare for the evening gown, Susan. Judges can see perspiration on your face-- or, worse, on your arms--under the lights. And you don't want that."
- "Now Susan, I don't put my suit on the night before, after it's been washed. You want your body to stretch it just so far as your body goes, but no more, so it's super tight when the judges see you."
- "You keep playing, Susan, whether you miss a note or skip a measure. I've had some baton tosses that were not quite perfect, but I didn't hesitate with the routine. Finish, finish, finish!"

Well, I knew that at least! And didn't her mentioning of exertion, stretching, mistakes make them more likely for someone trying this for the first time? Oooh, she was good at what she did, this smiling princess!

These incidental comments were not nearly as unsettling, though, as what she said at the end of the last session. Well, she didn't so much say it as hiss it.

We'd had our final walkthrough and were gathering our coats and purses from the auditorium seats before leaving. Mr. Pierce and the emcee were behind us, conferring up on the stage.

124

Mr. Pierce had also seemed particularly attentive to me this time, putting a hand on my shoulder to move me into a different position, asking if I needed any help with my music stand, wanting to make sure I was happy with my swimsuit. (We had no real "dress" rehearsal, by the way, always wearing everyday clothes.)

By chance Sally and I had put our things down next to each other, and I saw her glance toward the stage as she hiked her purse strap up over her shoulder. She had her baton in the other hand. She flashed a smile at the men on the stage, then turned to face me.

"You have a ride?" She knew I did.

"Oh, yes. The family car."

"Mm-hm. Let me walk you out." She put the arm with the baton behind me, ushering me up the aisle.

"Well, OK." I wondered if she might be going to give me, ever the neophyte in her view, some final words of advice about the competition. Or maybe, I thought, remembering what Sandy had said, she would explain how to handle Mr. Pierce. I could feel his eyes watching us, watching me. He had unnerved me a bit with his attention.

"You've come a long way, Suzie-Q," she began as we walked up the aisle side by side.

"Gee, thanks, Sally. You already know how to do all this stuff, though. You're sure to win." Suzie-Q?

"Oh, don't be silly. This is an open competition. Every one of the girls has just as good a chance to get the crown."

She looked around the entryway here, as if checking to see if anyone could overhear us. I think now she was being careful to follow the party line in public. Then we pushed through the double-doors together.

She walked me to the Rambler. When I had unlocked the door and turned back to say goodbye, she stepped in close beside me. Putting her lips to my ear and crossing my stomach with her baton, she said these words in a furious whisper:

"You win this pageant, bitch, and I'll carve my initials in that flat little tummy of yours with a kitchen knife."

Interlude: The Throne

I have a pretty darn good husband. He's considerate, faithful, dedicated to our children. But, like all men, he does have his blind spots. He was over the age of 40, for instance, before he came to understand completely one of the most basic elements of female lifestyle: the toilet seat.

Now, I know the toilet is often called a throne. When someone's had too much to drink, he or she can be said to be worshipping at the "Porcelain Throne." But I never fully recognized how the toilet is a place of power for men and women until this blind spot in my husband's vast learning was revealed to me just before our twentieth anniversary.

Fairfield's Miss Route 66 rarely sat on a throne, by the way. She stood on stage to receive the crown, and then her duties were to attend such events as the Phipps County Fair or the groundbreaking for a new municipal building. In some years the Christmas parade float did include a high seat for the town beauty. But none of those thrones was a toilet seat.

For the men of Fairfield, interestingly, there *was* an annual king on a commode. South Central Missouri State College's patron saint was Patrick, the legendary figure of Ireland. And on or near St. Pat's Day, March 17, the college crowned one of their students as the year's honorary monarch.

A vote was taken during the days leading up to the St. Pat's Day Weekend to select one student to

127

represent the saint at an evening ball and in an afternoon parade. He was installed as regent at the beginning of a rowdy procession that went from the bottom of Main Street the length of town to the college campus.

Because the student population at the college was nearly all male, and because they studied hard most weeks of the academic year, the celebration of St. Pat's was raucous, to say the least. Even though girlfriends came from across the state to spend the weekend, the Saturday afternoon celebration often got out of hand.

Students sat St. Pat on an old commode propped up on a manure cart, "borrowed" years ago from a county farm, and pulled him by hand in front of local businesses. There was always beer at this event (sometimes dyed green), and more than once local liquor stores were raided for additional drink.

The college's few coeds--and the town's wives, mothers, and daughters--knew to stay away on the afternoon of the celebration. Students lining the sidewalks of the route often were summoned by members of the unofficial court to bow down before St. Pat and seek his (drunken) blessing. Even respected professors were in danger of being dragged out of the crowd of bystanders and taken to pay their respects to St. Pat.

So, all this was definitely a male arena, a masculine rite with ironic trappings of empire. The symbolism of the event dismissed the feminine value of domestic order (the toilet, the bathroom) and asserted primitive rights of manhood (power, the outside world).

128

I was slow to perceive some of the links between toilets and gender in growing up, probably because I began my thinking with the fact that the scrubbers of the world are generally women. The wife or daughter has always been the bathroom cleaner of the average family. In wealthier homes the maid, not the valet, kneels before the toilet with her sponge and cleanser.

In the early years of my own marriage, it never occurred to either of us that my husband might clean the bathroom. But my man's blindness to the details of a woman's life went beyond that of most others of his gender.

One ground rule of American marriages after the institution of indoor plumbing, established early if not before the wedding, is that the toilet seat is to be left down when not in use. Although women must clean up the spatterings of men as well as any accidents of their own, their right to have the seat down is nearly universally accepted. Women getting up out of bed at night and visiting the bathroom in the dark do not want to sit in the bowl. The seat should be in place for the feminine derriere.

My husband, however, grew up in a masculine household, with one brother and no sisters. (It's true there was a mother, but she didn't really count in the fundamental shape of the Thornton household, even its bathroom.) His and his sibling's most frequent uses of the toilet were accomplished standing up. (I have reason to believe he washed his hands faithfully after completing his business, a practice not all men follow.) But he habitually left the toilet seat and toilet seat cover standing up, resting against the toilet tank in back.

After a week of being married to me (one-time aspirant for the crown of Miss Route 66), he left both seat and cover down after use, praising himself, of course, for unusual thoughtfulness.

But here's the distinction he never recognized in nineteen years of growing up at home and nearly another twenty married to me: the difference between toilet seat and toilet seat cover. When he first heard me say, "Leave the toilet seat down," he understood it as "leave everything above the bowl down." Seat and cover were a unit to him in this context, even though he divided them when occasion called for him to sit. Who can say why he didn't see two things--a seat and a cover. But he didn't.

While this was not perfect for me (who sometimes bounced her bottom on the cover at night), it was really not bad enough to correct. And we both became accustomed to the practice.

His epiphany about the divided nature of toilet construction came more than a decade after he made the more important discovery, as far as I'm concerned. He volunteered (that's right, volunteered!) to clean our bathrooms once a week for as long as we were married. (This is almost enough for me to stay married to him no matter what other faults he might have!)

If you're a woman, by the way, and you don't clean toilets regularly, there's something you won't see: the bottom of the toilet seat. It's down when you come in (given the considerate husband); it's down while you're there; it's down when you leave.

Without being too graphic, this can be a nice bit of blindness. Anything likely to be on the bottom of a toilet seat is not something you would be seeking. Since there's enough unpleasantness each of us has to confront in life, having a spouse spare you some difficulties is acceptable. (Of course, you have to return the favor in some other regard.)

I went a number of years appreciating the fact that my husband washed the bathrooms, and I came to forget over that long time what his efforts kept from my view. (I'm sure I don't have to tell you about the particular stomach flu that opened my eyes.)

It all goes to show that even thrones have ugly sides, I guess. And the second half of my story will show some of them.

I'm prepared as well to show them to the citizens of Fairfield tomorrow. Yes, I'm now ensconced in a room at the Fairfield Holiday Inn, writing out this account of adventures past and present on yellow legal pads. I'm also reviewing my speech for tomorrow. That's when the town holds its sesquicentennial celebration, which will include an elaborate recognition of the Miss Route 66 Pageant.

Something like a dozen former Misses Route 66 will be there, Blind Bill Martin (still the emcee) will tell of the winners' later successes, and town citizens will cheer this glorious history. They will, that is, until I step forward.

Of course, there have been changes in the pageant since my day. The women's movement did eventually reach even conservative communities like Fairfield, and candidates try to show less skin and more intelligence. But not that much, in my opinion.

The pageant survived for years, adapting to the times but still drawing its strength from men who want to look (and more) at girls' bodies. The winner is put on a figurative throne, surrounded by her court. But she's put there, I now know, to be kept out of the action as much as to be venerated.

The pageant produces an object, supposedly pure and beautiful. But most of the spectators older than the girls themselves know about ugly truths hidden beneath the tinsel, the fanfare, and even the girls' costumes. It's a conspiracy that has changed shape but not substance over the years.

So I say, tomorrow . . . let's flush it all down the toilet!

Volume Three: Discord. Chapter 1

When I told Sandy about Sally's threat at the final rehearsal for the Miss Route 66 Pageant, she was incredulous.

"She said that?"

"I'm not making it up." We were sitting at a booth in Fanny's Dairy Delite one afternoon during the week of the Pageant.

"A kitchen knife? You're sure she said she'd use a kitchen knife?" She held up a plastic spoon as if it were the item in question. We were both working on double-dip bowls of ice cream.

"I was thinking she'd tell me something about the competition, or maybe about Mr. Pierce. But this came out of nowhere. Carve her initials!"

"Well, now you know two things. One, she doesn't like you much. And, two, you must have some chance of winning this thing!"

I hadn't quite realized this second point. From the beginning I had had fantasies of winning. But the possibility that the judges would actually find me the best candidate, the genuine Miss Route 66, was, I thought, remote.

"Here's the real shocker," I told Sandy. She raised her eyebrows as I flipped a folded piece of fancy paper on the table between us.

"It looks like an invitation."

"Read it." And she did.

"A slumber party? On the night before the Pageant? Crazy!"

"I know. Sally's invited all the contestants, fourteen of us."

"You'd better skip this party. She's planning something. Maybe just to get everyone tired and baggy eyed."

That had been my original response. And I certainly wasn't going to let her come after me with a kitchen knife! But then I had begun to wonder. She couldn't do anything with Elizabeth and Mary and all the other girls there, could she? And I didn't really want to miss something big like this, a sleepover of all the potential Misses Route 66.

I looked over Sandy's shoulder and saw, behind the counter, the owners of Fanny's, Mrs. Hamilton and Miss Powers. They had been conferring thoughtfully about something, a business question, I guessed. Several times they had glanced over at us.

There was no separate kitchen at Fanny's, just open space beside and behind the two large soft ice cream makers. Counters, sinks, cabinets, and freezers provided places to work and to store the necessary machinery for this modest operation. Customers could see how things were made, if their orders were progressing, who was taking on which task.

"Now, Susan," said Sandy. "There's something I've been trying to tell you, but you've been so caught up in the contest, so busy. Actually, there are two things."

"Yeah? Is it about Mr. Pierce?"

"It's about Paul, Paul Thornton and your concert."

"OK. I haven't seen him since then, you know. I thought I might, on campus." I'd never worked up the courage to call him. Secretly, I'd hoped he'd call me. That would have confirmed that he was attracted to me. Otherwise I couldn't figure out why he'd been to hear me play the flute.

"Well, I'm the one who asked Paul to come to your house, but it was kind of by accident."

"Accident?"

"Yeah. You see, I really thought Larry might want to be there. He said you were interested in his worm . . . in, um, his science project."

"Oh, I don't know. I answered all his questions. But, after that, I didn't see him." Sandy had wanted me to think about dating Larry after I had successfully drifted away from Randy. I didn't dislike him, but his brother was surely the better looking one. But then I remembered the bracelet. Larry *had* shown an interest in me.

"Right," Sandy went on. "Anyway, I see Larry at church all the time, and, well, I thought I would invite him to come with me to hear you play."

"But Paul came. How did that happen?"

"See, what happened was this. I mentioned it to Mrs. Thornton, that there was this family flute concert and her son should come. I figured she'd know I was talking about Larry."

"So she told Paul to come? And he did. But why?"

"I guess he was just being polite, doing something for his mom. I don't know how it all got set up. But when I stopped by to get Larry, Paul came out of the house. I was too embarrassed to say anything. I just brought him along. He's nice enough."

Well, this was not encouraging, although it was still possible that Paul had actually jumped at the chance. Of course, the talk since then had been that he and Sally Winchester were definitely together. And he'd not done anything I was aware of to get in touch with me.

"Why are they looking at us, Sandy?" I said. I meant Fanny's two owners.

"Who?" She looked over her shoulder, seeing Mrs. Hamilton and Miss Powers. "Oh. I guess it's because I've started to work here. Actually, I go on in about ten minutes."

"What? Since when?"

"Um, last week, a week ago. You've been so busy with the pageant and all, I didn't have a chance to tell you about it. But I think it's going to be fun. These ladies are a stitch!"

Neither Sandy nor I had ever had a job other than baby-sitting. Our fathers didn't think their daughters would have to work once we were married. So there wasn't any reason to seek regular employment.

"So, what do you do?"

136

"Some of everything, it turns out. Make sandwiches, wait on customers, clean the booths."

"Hey, will you get free sundaes?"

"I get half-price. But I'll tell you what's neat--those two ladies who run Fanny's."

"Mrs. Hamilton and Miss Powers," I asserted.

"Well, 'Flora' and 'Madeline' to me," giggled Sandy. "They told me they don't 'stand on formalities.'" She poked her nose up in the air with her index finger, indicating stuck-up-ness.

"Your Dad's OK with this?"

"I convinced him the two old ladies would look after me, and he gave in. But I'm also figuring it's another way to see boys outside of school."

"Yeah," I agreed. "Hey, I'll come in to visit you and see the guys, too."

"OK, but I'm the one who's wearing the tight white skirt and bumping my rump!"

I laughed. And then she went through the gate in the counter to get her apron and start her shift. I wasn't due home for another half hour, so I stayed in the booth, musing over what Sandy had told me, what Sally was up to, what Mr. Pierce wanted.

It sure looked like my dreams of Paul Thornton were over. And Larry's pursuit, with bracelet, was something more definite I would have to deal with. Maybe Sally would announce that she and Paul were going steady at her slumber party this weekend. That would seal it for me!

There was also Mr. Pierce, the two-faced pageant consultant. He seemed all smiles and encouragement at meetings and rehearsals. But if he got you alone, another side surfaced. A side I didn't understand and didn't want to confront.

In my imagination I tried to follow through where his glass fingering would lead. I remembered the sensations I felt whenever I followed Juliet's instructions--"Pet me." It made me shiver. He was a grown man, someone like my father, with his own kids.

I saw Sandy now at the counter where orders were placed. She gave me a little wave, holding aloft a stubby pencil and an ordering pad.

She had something here, I realized: a job that would last longer than the Miss Route 66 contest (unless, of course, I won). She could work through the summer, before she went off to college (tiny Tarkeo College in the northwest corner of the state). She might be starting something that would grow and develop throughout her life. What was I doing trying to win one little contest?

2

Whether in the end I won or lost the Miss Route 66 crown, I was still, I found, developing new stature. I felt it most when I was in the presence of Blind Bill Martin, the event's emcee.

Now, you're saying, the emcee of this event couldn't see?! And it's true. Bill Martin had been blind since birth, and the beauty contestants were to him voices and an occasional hand touching his arm or shoulder.

But Blind Bill also had a "photographic" memory (I know it's not the right word!). And, once he had been told the names of the contestants and heard them speak, he began to build an understanding of their personalities that was, it turned out, as sharp as that of any seeing person.

Learning where each would stand at the beginning of the pageant, he could direct each of us through the entire event. His tone and manner made it clear he knew which of us he was speaking to, which of us had spoken to him.

As often seems to be the case, this man who had lost one sense had superior talents in other areas. Bill Martin possessed unusual musical ability. He could play any manner of string instrument by ear, and he sang in a nasal, raspy baritone that had made him a local country and western star for three decades. You could hear his show every weekday morning on KPPR, Fairfield's one radio station.

He'd been announcing winners at this beauty pageant ever since one not altogether sensitive Fairfield mayor had asserted that a blind man was the perfect unbiased host. And he sang our version of "Miss America" ("Miss Route Sixty-Six") with a twang that would probably have destroyed Bob Barker's sensibility, had he ever heard it.

I liked Blind Bill immediately because he never questioned my legitimacy as a Miss Route 66 candidate. Perhaps it was my feeling of inferiority, but, until Sally Winchester made her knife threat, I'd felt that most of the folks involved in the pageant were just humoring me.

"Susan Bell?" Blind Bill said to me when we were introduced by Mary Dunkin. "You're the flute player, right?" he said.

"Um, yes. I am." How did he know?

"Do you play by ear?" he asked, then chuckled. "I--heh, heh--can't read a note." Can't read. Um-hum, I get it.

"Mostly, I just play what's on the page. My Mom, who's teaching me, can play any tune she's heard. But I'm getting better at that too."

"Good for you. Not much flute music in what I do, but I'm looking forward to hearing you play."

I felt a little awkward talking to Mr. Martin. I wondered if I should stand where his eyes, behind dark glasses, would be directed at me. Or maybe, if he seemed to be cocking his head, I should address the ear on the side closer to me.

"I hope you like it. I've . . . uh . . . your music. . . ."

140

"Now, you don't have to pretend with me. I'm more popular with the senior square dance set than with you young people. But you may be surprised to find out how much we have in common. I mean, we're both musicians. And I guess we're both pretty!"

He laughed, and it made me laugh too.

Later Mary explained that the best way to get along with Blind Bill was to just act as if he was like everyone else.

"He has his ways of getting around," she asserted. He used a cane, which we would hear tapping about behind stage as we walked through our numbers in rehearsals. "And he doesn't forget anything."

"I think I already like him!"

As rehearsals continued, Blind Bill seemed to single me out as a companion, someone to take a break with. Perhaps he sensed my nervousness as a newcomer to the event, wanting to reassure me.

And maybe he shared my uncertainty about Sally.

"I have trouble understanding that girl," he told me one time when we were waiting for a contestant to repair her hula hoop. "Ever since her first time in the pageant--oh, some years ago--she hasn't spoken clearly. There's always some *shhh* and *sss* in her speech." He made a hissing sound.

"Really? I hadn't noticed."

"She's got a pretty face, though, right?"

"Oh, yes." I agreed, but looking more closely from time to time, I wasn't quite as sure as I used to be.

There was a certain hardness to Sally's look, a fixed expression. It was disguised by her bright smile, all those clean white teeth. But when the smile ended, her mouth and chin and cheeks seemed to fall back into a peculiar rigidity.

"You and me," said Bill, patting my arm. "We get along."

I'm sure I also liked taking breaks with Blind Bill Martin because that kept me away from Mr. Pierce. These two men had worked together for some years and apparently had had no disagreements. They had separate spheres of responsibility and generally were in different places.

Mr. Pierce was strictly behind the scenes, making arrangements (the small orchestra that provided music had to be paid), getting the stage ready (this year our theme was Paradise, so the set represented the Garden of Eden), choreographing events (where we walked, posed, waited).

And Blind Bill was the voice at the front of the stage that guided participants and audience on the night of the pageant itself. He would charm family and friends in the opening minutes, introduce the contestants in each area of competition, announce the narrowing field of finalists until we all arrived at a single Miss Route 66.

Never clashing over territory, the two men performed their tasks well, bringing many elements together into an impressive (given our small-town small-time-iness) night of entertainment for the residents of Fairfield.

142

As we neared the pageant (and the slumber party that was to precede it), I thought I might be able to ask Mary Dunkin about Mr. Pierce. She had guided me through the process with hints gained from experience, not the kind of demoralizing suggestions Sally was always coming up with.

"Mr. Pierce seems to be especially nice to Sally, don't you think? I mean, he does assume she's the winner."

"It's not just that," Mary said. She looked over at the pageant's Senior Consultant and this year's frontrunner. They were making sure her high baton tosses wouldn't get tangled in the ropes that raised curtains and props.

"What do you mean?"

"Well, he's nice to all the girls. You know the joke about the traveling salesman?"

"Which one?" I couldn't remember any right then, though I'd certainly heard some. That Mary would know some risqué jokes as well as Shakespeare surprised me.

"The traveling salesman's truck breaks down," she began, looking around to make sure no one had come close enough to hear. "And he asks a farmer if he can spend the night in the barn."

"Of course."

"You can picture the traveling salesman in a nice suit and tie, the farmer in overalls. He's a bit of a hayseed."

I thought of him as a hillbilly, an image the rest of the nation still has of Ozark country folk.

"The farmer's daughter is beautiful, of course," I noted. I did know the genre.

"Yes. Stunning and . . . " (in a whisper) " . . . stacked!"

In my mind's eye the salesman appeared in the form of Mr. Pierce. And the daughter was Sally.

"So the farmer says, 'You can sleep the night in the barn, but stay away from my daughter when she comes to milk the cow in the morning.'"

"Um-hm." My attention shifts to the farmer's daughter. Has she been waiting for just such an opportunity? A good-looking city man to run away with. Does she already know what he wants to do? Has she been practicing in her bedroom how she would respond when the traveling salesman invited her up in the hayloft?

"When the farmer awakes," concluded Mary, "the salesman, the car, the girl, *and the cow* have been gone for hours!"

3

Two days before Sally's slumber party, Larry Thornton stopped me in the hall at school to report that he'd won the science fair competition.

"Congratulations! So you'll go to the regional fair in Jefferson City?"

"That's right. Me and my worms." Once again a funny little smile played around his eyes.

"*And* your data. I mean, you couldn't have done it without all us dumb worm-haters who filled out your questionnaires and proved the public's ignorance."

"True. Let me thank you once again." He took a stiff bow. "The cause of science thanks you, too."

Larry's eyes were, I noticed, conspicuously focused on my tummy. I was wearing slacks that fit snugly, and a light knit top under an unbuttoned sweater hugged my midsection. I shifted my weight from one foot to the other, tick-tocking my hips.

"Do your worms live that long?" I asked. "So long that they can make it until February?"

"Oh, not the same worms. The great-great-great grandchildren of the worms you petted months ago." His eyes bounced up from my belly to my face, but then wandered back down again.

"Hey, I didn't pet them! I just looked at one as he crawled all around on you." I made a face and gave a mock shiver, remembering the slimy-looking, brown creature squirming on Larry's fingers, reaching for the dirt, its home. After the shiver I sucked my tummy in even more. "And don't tell me again about their disgusting reproductive habits."

I was really just joking here, trying to keep the conversation light while watching to see where his eyes were directed. Too, I was hoping to figure a way to return that charm bracelet with its cute little musical instruments he had given me. So much time had passed since he'd done it that I didn't even know how to bring it up.

"It's not any more disgusting than the reproductive habits of other creatures, even humans," said Larry seriously. Now his gaze stayed on my face.

This was hard. I wasn't prepared for an earnest talk about human reproduction with a boy. How had I let the conversation wander to this subject?

"So, you still work at the worm farm, even though you're getting ready to make some scientific breakthrough?"

"Sure, I'm saving for college. I hope to get a scholarship, but, even if I do, I'll want pocket money."

"Yeah. Did you know Sandy's working at the Dairy Delite? She's getting experience."

"That's good. What about you?"

"Just . . . you know, practicing the flute, and, um, the beauty contest." I remembered his brother's coming to my first little recital, which had been a dry run for my pageant performance. Larry had been accidentally excluded. I wouldn't have invited him, but I also wouldn't have prevented him from being there when Sandy invited him.

"Why don't you come see the worm farm with me sometime?" he asked. "It's neat after dark."

"How so?" I wondered if this might be the chance to return the bracelet. I'd have to do so without offending.

"I've got to work tomorrow night for a couple of hours," he went on. "I'll show you."

"Well. . . ." I guess I could stand another hour's lecture on worms, especially if it ended with his gift returned.

"I'll pick you up around 8 o'clock," Larry said, taking my hesitation for acquiescence. "You need something to keep your mind off the contest anyway."

There was some truth to what Larry said about pressure, so I accepted his proposal.

I had been pleased with myself all along for taking the step of entering this contest. And throughout the early meetings and rehearsals I'd stayed quite calm about it all. But it had been like an exercise to this point, preparation for something off there in the future that I hadn't fully seen myself doing.

Now the event was just a few days away. Instead of empty seats out in a dark auditorium there would be a live audience--family, friends, strangers. Judges would scrutinize my clothes, my stance, my every move. This theory I'd entertained that I was a new person was going to be put to a real test, under lights.

This was one of the few times I actually wished Tricia were here to help me. She had put herself in front of the public so many times. How did she do it? All those people looking at her. What did it feel like? How did she keep her composure?

Years later, of course, I've come to recognize that it wasn't so easy for her either. All those trips to the bomb shelter were a way of evading boys, sure. But they also meant escape from being on display to anyone who attended the plays she was in. She knew she was an object, something others possessed as they held her in view. In their minds they could make her what they wanted; they could define her. She'd had to learn how to survive such public examination.

When I looked at myself head-on in Tricia's mirror, I was both subject and object, the viewer as well as the thing viewed. I could only be so harsh in such a self-examination.

Even when I was critical of my stance, my modest breasts, my plain face, I still couldn't forget the thoughts, worries, and dreams that were inside the person standing there. I knew the story behind every expression, the reasons leading to each gesture, the hopes inspiring any move.

I was, that is, not an Other separate from a Self, and this posing was not the same as subjecting myself to a truly critical analysis.

"Hello there," said Tricia's pet parrot.

"Juliet, Juliet," I asked. "Who am I to you?"

"Pretty bird," she offered.

I turned sideways, examining again my body's long, lean profile, the slender frame and flat belly that had dazed Randy Alexander months ago. In my mind's eye, I tried to imagine being pregnant, my middle swelling out. I arched my back and pushed out with my stomach.

But I couldn't really think of myself as a mother, as a woman who produces babies. I wasn't ready to nurture another soul with my own soul so fragile, just emerging.

"The Mother Road," I thought. America's highway giving birth to dreams, feeding new generations with hopes. If I were to become Miss Route 66, wouldn't I have to do something like that?

Well, probably not. The acts of Miss Route 66 were hardly so noble. Pose with the mayor, stand nearby as the first spadeful of earth is dug for a new municipal parking lot, wave at the crowds streaming into the Phipps County Fair in July.

No, all I had to do was be pretty. (Not just sweet, but pretty.) I turned back to look head-on into the mirror.

Was this someone who could attract men? Randy, yes. Larry, perhaps. Paul, apparently not. Mr. Pierce, yes.

I thought again about the look in the eyes of our assistant principal when he'd sat opposite me at Fanny's Dairy Delite. The unfocused gaze, the drool at the corner of his mouth, the finger on the rim of the Coke glass. Ugh!

I saw my own fingers there in the glass before me. They ran up my sides, and then down. They touched my breasts. They passed across my belly. They went further.

A funny thing had happened along the road toward the final event of the Miss Route 66 competition. After having worried and worried that my own pleasure was sinful, I'd discovered recently that the sense of guilt that had been haunting me was waning.

This was good--or, more likely bad--in some abstract moral code, I knew. But in my heart it was causing less and less sting.

I asked Juliet. "Is it really wrong? Should I stop? Will it hurt me?"

"Pet me," she answered once again.

Did I deserve petting? Should I provide myself pleasure? Was I an object to myself, or was a deeper voice within me telling me simply that I was worthy of pleasure?

4

When did young girls of that era discuss such matters as physical pleasure? A slumber party with a few close friends would be the perfect opportunity for talk to turn to sex. But the truth would be hard to find in so much giggling, a few exaggerated claims, much guesswork derived from little experience.

The slumber party I was headed for, with the other Miss Route 66 contestants, would be even less likely to answer my most pressing questions. We didn't know each other that well, and our one overriding interest, the Pageant, would probably be the main topic of conversation. I might, however, learn some more about Mr. Pierce.

Sandy Johnson, as my best friend in the neighborhood and at school, was the one person who might reveal her own secrets to me in this area, if I was willing to be open first. I stopped by Fanny's Dairy Delite to see if we could talk.

"Let me tell you about ice cream," Sandy said as soon as she had a break and could join me in a booth.

"I know about ice cream."

"Oh, you only think you do. For instance, when was it invented?"

"Invented? Hm."

"Yeah! Well, it's probably as old as the Middle Ages. Knights and all used snow with salt in it to cool their drinks. Most drinks had fruit, but some also included milk or cream. So probably the first ice cream came along back then."

"OK, that's interesting. But I want to talk about something else." I could see Sandy had gotten into her work.

"Of course, a big breakthrough came in the late 1920s with electricity and mechanical refrigeration. The average dairy plant was soon manufacturing hard ice cream. And now, Americans probably eat more than twelve pounds of ice cream apiece every year. We might be as famous for our ice cream as for democracy."

"Oh, I don't know about that."

"Listen, I'm telling you some things you might need to know when you're Miss Route 66." She leaned forward and tapped my Coke glass with her plastic spoon.

"You think I'm going to give speeches about ice cream?"

"I think you need to know that it's important to Route 66."

"How so?"

"Places like this, Fanny's Dairy Delite, they're part of what traveling down the highway is all about. People have to stop, and they need something to eat or drink when they do."

I could see that she had a point. Especially in the hot summers, when families took that vacation trip to see the American West, they could suffer from the heat. We local kids stopped there too, of course, on our regular cruising about town.

"OK, I give you that. Are you learning all this from your bosses?"

I had never really thought much about Mrs. Flora Hamilton, the retired nurse, and Miss Madeline Powers, former teacher. They'd been running this shop for as long as I could remember, and my friends and I had been coming here ever since we had permission to travel about town on our own. But I didn't know who these two ladies were or what went into the operation they ran.

"Flora is the one who has learned how to make ice cream, the machines and all. Madeline keeps track of the books, the business regulations, permits. They're sharp ladies."

"How long have they been running the place?"

"Since the early 50s. Madeline realized people would be traveling more then. I guess, because the war was over and all."

She had been right, of course. The postwar boom, returning soldiers, and a confidence in our country had inspired journeys to new places and holiday travel down the Mother Road.

The women had chosen a nondescript building, a metal shed with a rounded roof, alongside the highway. When they opened, it had been on the edge of town and along the main route of travelers. Now the town had grown out around them, and their address was on Business Route 66. But, as Sandy later told me, the proprietresses had put up enough billboards on the approaches to Fairfield that they had regular traffic most of the year and did a heavy business throughout the summer months.

For their publicity campaign, they had decided they needed a logo, a distinctive emblem. Madeline drew the outline of a motherly figure to be their "Fanny." And that figure of a slightly stout, cheerful matron sporting an apron and waving a welcome appeared on the big sign mounted above the door and on dozens of billboards along Route 66 to the east and west.

"The secret to their success, though," said Sandy, "is their ice cream itself."

Fanny's sold soft-serve ice cream, what was sometimes called "Ice Milk" in those days. And now that I think back, it was about the only place in my early childhood where you could get soft ice cream. Kids loved to watch it pour out of the machine's nozzle and fill up a cone, then form that multiple-bulbed tower above the cone, topped with a twirling tail. (My Dad, of course, preferred the old-fashioned, regular ice cream, insisting that the new stuff was for sissies.)

"I bet you're going to tell me how they make it," I admitted.

"Sure. It's a good story."

"Since I can't stop you," I laughed, "go ahead."

"Flora explained it to me. At one point--I don't know--twenty-five years ago, some people in the business were using small freezers. They would freeze a specific amount of ice cream during one operation and then fill again for the next batch."

"OK." I was glad Sandy had a new interest here, but I wasn't sure I needed to know all this detail. Maybe she should sit down with Larry and hear about worms for a while!

"Anyway, these batch freezers were a key step along the way to soft ice cream. Some bright guy eventually figured out that this type of equipment could be used to eliminate the hand dipping of ice cream. Just let it be made in the freezer and then poured right out of the freezer before it got completely solid."

"So you like working here?" I gestured around the shop, at the ice cream makers behind the counter. I was familiar with the silver cylindrical bodies of the two freezers, each with a spigot on the bottom--kind of like a beer keg on its side.

"Yeah. Wait a minute. Let me finish. See, what they came up with was a dispensing freezer, one that froze the ingredients inside the machine. The stuff wasn't as hard, of course, as regular ice cream, but it held its shape long enough to be eaten."

"I think it tastes better," I admitted. In fact, hard ice cream freezes my mouth, and I often stop enjoying the flavor after a half dozen bites.

"Hand-dipped ice cream is also hard to scoop. And for someone feminine like me," Sandy smiled and patted her hair. "For someone feminine like me, soft ice cream is much better."

Tricia and I had bent spoons at home trying to carve out bowlfuls. And my father always frowned when we banged our spoons into our bowls, trying to cut through those rigid blocks. With the soft stuff you could just lick with your tongue and get as much as a spoon would dig out of the other kind.

Of course, you could let regular ice cream soften by leaving it out of the freezer for a while, before or after you served it. But, as kids, we seldom had the necessary foresight or patience.

"Now the knock against soft-serve ice cream is that it's not as good for you," Sandy went on. "It's not got all the stuff regular ice cream does, they say."

"I think it tastes as good."

"Well, it is a complete food with carbohydrates, minerals, and vitamins. It doesn't have as much fat or sugar as regular ice cream, and it's higher in protein."

I had to laugh. She was sounding like a commercial, or a recent convert.

Still, I'd sought her out today to ask about something else and had gotten nowhere in that endeavor. Yes, ice cream satisfied a certain craving. And the act of eating definitely gave pleasure. But what about the craving inspired by Juliet's order, "Pet me"? Was doing that as good for you as eating soft ice cream? And exactly what was Mr. Pierce craving?

5

The next night I followed through on my promise to let Larry show me the secrets of worm farming. But when he picked me up at my house, I had the charm bracelet tucked inside my jacket pocket and a plan to return it.

This evening with worms stands out in my memory many years later, a landmark on my romantic journey. I learned I had a serious suitor. But the whole night also had an eerie feeling to it, largely because we did what we did pretty much in the dark.

Another part of that surreal feeling I experienced was no doubt a reflection of the tension I was feeling about Sally's sleepover the next evening and about the pageant competition.

Underlying my apprehension about these events was the unsettling figure of Mr. Pierce and his scary proposal. I worried that, somehow, he'd get me off to the side during the pageant and resume his offer. Or before the show he'd find me alone in a dressing room. I imagined him popping up unexpectedly, just when I wouldn't be ready to deal with him.

As Larry and I pulled into the parking lot of Dr. Staff's Bait Garden, I wondered why in the world I had added one more difficult event to this week! Why was I letting him take one step closer to a date with me? Why didn't I just tuck that stupid bracelet away in my sock drawer and pretend nothing had ever happened?

"I'm not going to turn on the lights," Larry said, opening the car door for me. He held up a flashlight with tissue paper over the end, generating a glow but not a precise beam of light. "We want to sneak up on these worm guys while they're active."

"They're nocturnal?"

"Not exactly, but they tend to stay out of the light."

The worm farm was a low cinder-block building, square and squat on a dead-end street at the south end of town. The nearest streetlight was a block away, so, once the car's headlights had been extinguished, I could make out only shadowy shapes around me.

"What you're coming to see, remember, are Lumbricus Terrestris," Larry explained. Now he was whispering, as if the worms might hear us approaching.

I remembered they had a Latin name that began with "L," but that's as much as I had retained from his science project questionnaire. "Yes, the care and feeding of Lumbricus Terrestris," I confirmed.

He unlocked the door and swung it open. "A rule of thumb," he whispered, "is one square yard of surface for every 1,000 nightcrawlers. They get their oxygen from the surface."

A "rule of thumb." It made me think of the demonstration worm that had been squirming on Larry's fingers the day he explained his science

158

project. Unfortunately, it also brought to mind Mr. Pierce's finger on a Coke glass. And Randy's mouth organ.

"They jump into the air to breathe like porpoises or whales?" I asked, my nervousness making me into a joker, a clown.

"No. The oxygen works its way into the soil. But that's why it can't be too deep. We use these plastic pickle buckets." I could see the floor was covered with twenty-gallon buckets arranged in orderly rows.

"Pickles?"

"Staff gets them at a reduced rate from a pickle factory in Texas. Don't ask me how. Anyway, we fill them with moist peat moss, up to a depth of 6 to 7 inches. Then add the worms."

"They're all for bait, right? Fishermen?

"Right. They spit on them for luck, the fishermen. Did you know that?"

"No. I guess it's better than kissing them." Now, why did I say that? This wasn't a topic I wanted to be bringing up on a dark night in an empty building on a dead-end street!

"Or eating them," Larry added with a soft laugh. "But we have to feed them, not eat them. Let's take a look."

He propped the flashlight up on a shelf so one row of buckets was dimly illuminated. Then he picked up a large sack and a hand scoop.

"This is called 'laying mash.' You get it from the feed store. It's higher in protein than chicken starter, so the worms like it better."

I wasn't really following him in this explanation. But I assumed he was adding to the soil the same thing you might feed chickens. I recalled that he'd told me how worms would eat the rotten pear mush in my neighborhood. Larry sprinkled a thin layer over the soil in each bucket and then lightly sprayed the mash with water from a hose.

"The water makes it easier for the worms to consume the food. You'll see them start moving in a minute," he whispered and went to get the flashlight.

"Don't you mix the food in with the soil, where they can get at it easier?"

"Oh, no. You'll get 'protein poisoning' in your soil, and you'll find your worms dying in a matter of days. It's acid buildup."

"I guess there is a science to this."

"That's why you don't harvest worms after feeding, but before. You let them eat up what's in the soil, then take them."

"Speaking of giving things to worms and all, I. . . ."

I was about to say, "I have something for you," meaning the bracelet. But I realized this would sound more like "I have a gift for you," something to match the bracelet.

So I said instead, "I, um, have to give you credit for . . . taking care of these worms so well. Of course, they're all headed for a fish's gullet."

"They have a full life before that," he countered. "Watch this." He motioned me over to another row of buckets, ones to which he hadn't added the laying mash.

"Every ten days, we toss the beds. It gets air in there. What was on the top goes to the bottom, and vice versa."

Larry took a miniature pitchfork and dug into three or four of the buckets, turning the soil over and, I assume, lifting worms up into the air. The light was fainter here away from the flashlight.

"We bore small holes in the sides of the buckets before we put the worms in there, but this gives them much more of what they need. It has to be absorbed through their skin, the oxygen."

"OK. Yes, you're good to them." I was stuck on this track, but still trying to figure out a way to bring up the bracelet.

"Now watch," he said. And he cut on a bright overhead light.

I looked over his shoulder into one of the buckets and saw that the soil was still moving, though he was no longer turning it with his little fork. It was like a simmering stew or some dark volcanic lake, moving toward a rolling boil or settling down after an eruption.

"Ooh! They're moving in there."

"Yes, trying to get away from the light. They want to be down under the surface. Look at them through this glass."

He had a large, hand-held magnifying glass, probably something he'd used in his science project. He stepped aside so I could have a closer look, putting one arm around my waist to usher me forward.

I gasped with surprise at what I saw magnified to ten times its original size. It was a sea of snake bodies, writhing and twisting, arching and dipping. There were so many tangled up together than I didn't see heads or tails--and couldn't have told the difference between them! The peat moss under the glass resembled a gravel pit, though the worms moved through it so easily the individual pieces seemed light, like cardboard or plastic. It might have been a magician's potion or the intertwining fingers of a hundred hidden spell casters.

"Neat, huh?" asked Larry with genuine earnestness.

"Wow!" was all I could come up with.

But I took one more look anyway, perhaps to show I had not been frightened by what he was showing me. The teeming mass of worms and earth and mash was like some elemental soup of creation, the beginning of all living things, a reproductive soup.

"Susan," asked Larry. "Will you go out with me?"

6

I'm not sure why I agreed to the date with Larry. Partly, I felt guilty that Paul had been invited to my concert in his place. Too, I still had the bracelet Larry had given me, and I felt I should acknowledge the gift in some way. And maybe I was starting to appreciate his work ethic, his commitment to taking projects through to completion.

But probably most of all I was just worn down by all the things that were building toward climaxes in my life: the pageant competition; Sally's threat and the slumber party; Mr. Pierce's advances. Why not have something to take advantage of after all these things were over? Who wouldn't want an interested young man to take her to the movies, buy her a soda, pay her compliments? This was not a bad thing to have in your future, especially if you were going to lose a beauty contest.

You see, my confidence had started to sag a bit in the last few days. There had been too many sessions in front of the mirror in Tricia's room. And perhaps Sandy's projected career as an ice cream historian/manufacturer was beginning to make more sense to me than my imagined life as a beauty contest queen.

I did tell Larry our date would have to be the following weekend, since I had the competition on Saturday. He agreed, offering to help me at the pageant, though, if needed. And he promised to be out in the auditorium rooting for me. I wasn't unhappy to have more than my parents in a little fan club.

My mother's support of a blossoming new me had been evident ever since she first realized the flute resting on her dining room table was not the property of one of my friends, but instead my very own purchase. While she didn't think I had to win the pageant, she did want me to develop my musical ability. All through the preliminaries, she spent time every day critiquing my solo and helping me with the outfits I would wear.

My father, though, seemed even more distant than usual in this process. I had assumed it was his work, the regular pressures of business. But it turns out there were other factors leading to his current state of mind.

Before I headed off for Sally's and the fateful slumber party, I found him out in the back yard holding a golf club.

"You're taking up golf?" I asked with obvious surprise. I had been carrying an overnight case out to the Rambler.

He looked up at me and grinned shyly. "Well now, I might. Don't you think I could?"

"Well, sure you could, I guess. If you wanted to. But, I don't know, you don't seem the type."

He held up a hand, waved me back a step. Then he settled himself into a golfer's stance, though there was no ball teed up for him to hit. He took a swing, and I saw immediately it was the stroke of someone

164

who knew what he was doing. His middle-aged paunch, though, didn't belong with the easy swing.

"I've played this game," he offered simply.

"I can see! But I never knew that." I set my bag down.

"Yes. It was some years ago." He sighed, recalling, I suppose, that earlier time. "But I've been feeling out of shape recently. And I wondered if I took up golf again, could I lose a little of this extra weight." He patted his pear-shaped middle.

"Did you learn to play when you were in high school?" I asked. And that prompted him to explain something I'd never known. He had played golf, oddly, in the war.

My father had served with the Signal Corps in England during World War II, getting some of the training that would inspire his civilian career later. His several years on a base in the countryside near Newcastle had been a mixture, 95 parts tedium and five parts serious danger. Communications centers were always targets for Nazi air raids, but his unit was small enough that it escaped heavy, repeated bombardment.

And for the months before and after D-Day, his tour settled into a surreal routine of logging communication data related to the aerial bombing of the German army on the Continent and learning, of all things, the game of golf.

The threat of air raids was always highest at night, and so his most regular shifts were from late afternoon to midnight or from midnight to midmorning. In the calmer daylight hours he and some others took up the sport.

There was a modest nine-hole course near the base, open to GIs stationed in the area. And he and several buddies played a round nearly every day, all using the same set of secondhand clubs they had purchased collectively in the village.

"I can remember every hole on that course," he told me laughing. "The par-three's and the par-five's, the sand traps, the high rough. It was an awfully well-designed course for such an out-of-the-way place. And pretty country, not that far from the coast. No one playing but the elderly and off-duty troops."

I had not played any sports outside of neighborhood softball myself. And I knew few girls who took sports seriously. Elizabeth Rogers, the Miss Route 66 contestant and Fairfield High's best female athlete, was unusual for the time. Sports just wasn't something most of us did once we'd entered puberty. Except for cheerleading or baton twirling or dancing, we avoided strenuous physical activity.

"What's the fun of golf?" I asked my dad.

"Hmm," he thought a minute, using the club as a cane to lean on. "I think it has to do with the round you play. Now some people think it's the hole-in-one you're after, the great single stroke. But not me, not that one great shot. I like the rhythm and progress of the whole round, playing each hole and adding to your score. Then, at the end, you've taken a little journey."

"OK."

166

"Every nine holes is a combination of odd situations and challenges. What you have to do is put them all together into a single experience, the round you play that day. There's a total of strokes-- as close to par as you can--but in that total is a process that goes from beginning through middle to end."

"I bet you were pretty good!" I offered. He smiled. "It's kind of how I feel playing a concert."

He thought a minute. "I can see that. But in England, in the war, it might even have been more, um, satisfying, in a funny sort of way."

"How's that?"

"There was the war, you see, in the background all the time. We had air raids and our own planes going out. Most of the time enemy bombers were flying past us, going after more important targets. But they were always there. And for some months we worried about an invasion, so there were drills, alerts. There were even some pretty terrible scenarios we had to consider."

Dad had gotten a funny, faraway look in his eyes as he remembered. He'd never told me much about his time in England.

"And in some ways it seemed like the war would never end. We'd keep bombing, and they'd keep bombing. My buddies and I kept tracking the communication, before and after D-Day."

"Yeah."

"But in the pauses of the war, mostly through the middle of the day, we'd play golf. Me and Freddy and Josh and Sam mostly, a foursome. It was outside, pretty country like I said. Separate from our work, from the war. And it had its own enclosed, finished feel, something we started, continued, completed."

I recalled my father's courtship of my mother, the proposal by telephone. He had shown a certain flair in using the material of his profession to reach his ladylove. And he lit up now, talking of this almost forgotten experience, of fellowship and pleasure and accomplishment. What had happened to his energy and enthusiasm since then?

In the years of his children's growing up, the force of his personality seemed to have evaporated, leaving him a balding, overweight, middle-aged man slumped in an easy chair before the television set. I can see now that he had begun to realize how stale and uneventful his life had become. He'd concluded that returning to golf might also bring back the same spirit he'd possessed as a young man.

It was many days later that I realized his immediate inspiration for change came from seeing change in his wife.

7

The slumber party at Sally Winchester's was mostly fun, despite an underlying tension that, I think, all the girls felt.

We were, after all, competitors for the same crown, and there was always the feeling that, if you admitted something or revealed something, it might give others an advantage.

The whole event also had a somewhat disjointed feel to it, coming in stages that didn't follow one after the other. I think this had to do with Sally's plan for the night and what seemed to be a minor rebellion by the other girls in the form of an energetic pillow fight.

The first phase of the evening was dinner. Mrs. Winchester brought out trays of tuna and chicken salad sandwiches and a huge bowl of a fine German potato salad. There was ice cream for dessert, which we all wanted to decline, thinking of those extra pounds going into our swimsuits the next day. But the party atmosphere won out, and most of us figured we'd burn off extra calories with nervousness. anyway.

Then the games began--charades with four teams. Sally had arranged the groups, and I was surprised that she'd put herself with some of the weaker players. I had assumed she would want to win here, as with the pageant tomorrow. But she and her partners were the slowest at guessing even easy ones like "Jail House Rock," "Wake Up, Little Suzie," and *Gone With the Wind*.

Whether giving the clues or guessing, Sally was repeatedly off the mark, but entertainingly so. She squealed at her mistaken conclusions, laughed at her own inept hints, whooped in praise of the other teams. In the end she insisted on a mock award ceremony, giving everyone a party favor for playing, even her own losing group.

Her parents left us to go to bed about 11 o'clock, but of course nobody was prepared to sleep right away. Somebody called for ghost stories, and Sally turned off most of the lights. We were scattered about the family's spacious den, some on sofas, others on camping cots, a few on easy chairs pushed together. Mary Dunkin said she knew a good scary story.

"This girl was at home alone one night. Her parents had gone to a party at the country club that would linger into the wee hours of the morning."

"Uh-oh," one of the other girls said.

"Turn on all the lights," cautioned another.

"That girl should call her boyfriend right now," a third insisted.

Mary went on. "Everything was fine until she shut off the TV and got ready to go up to bed."

"She heard a noise in the basement?"

"There was a scratching at the door?"

"The phone went dead?"

170

"No," Mary said, looking around mysteriously at the faces peering out from the darkness. "No, it was worse than that! Standing at the foot of the stairs, she heard moaning, someone in pain. 'Oh-oh-oh-oo-oooh!' It sounded like someone who was sick or hurt bad. 'Oh-oh-oh-oo-oooh!' And it came from the master bedroom! 'Oh-oh-oh-oo-oooh!'"

"Don't go up there!"

"There's a murderer in the house!"

"Call the police!"

"She stopped at the foot of the stairs and listened." As Mary talked, her voice got softer and softer. So we all leaned toward her to hear. "The moaning got worse. It was terrible! 'Oh-oh-oh-oo-oooh!'"

I could see girls pulling covers around them, pairs holding hands. Mary seemed to shiver herself.

"'Who's there?' the girl asked in a timid little voice. The moaning stopped." Mary paused. We were all still. "Then it came again, 'Oh-oh-oh-oo-oooh!'"

I saw eyes wide around the room, girls holding their breath.

"'Who's there?' she asked and started up the stairs, one step at a time. One step. Two steps. Three steps."

"No!"

"Go back down!"

"Run!"

"Top step!" Mary announced. We all held our breath. When she suddenly spoke out in a loud, husky voice, pretending to be a man, we all jumped. "It's just your mother, sweetie. We've been doing that new dance, the dirty dog, and she likes it!"

And that led to an immediate pillow fight, several girls swinging at Mary, who was convulsed with laughter.

I teamed up with Liz Rogers in the melee, I guess because she was sitting beside me when the first blow was struck. We tried to protect each other and sometimes attacked in tandem. It was all in fun, of course. No one gets hurt in a pillow fight, although, if a pillow breaks, there's a mess to clean up.

The odd thing about it was that the girls ended up pounding Sally, burying her under a dozen pillows. I thought it a victory for us underdogs, an expression of our resentment that she had the title sewn up. But the next day I learned that the pillow fight had actually gone precisely according to Sally's plan.

After it was all over, I found myself lying beside Liz. As most of the other girls finally began to drift off for a few hours of sleep before dawn, she and I talked over what was to happen tomorrow evening. Although she was younger than I, she had had more experience in beauty contests. So I listened carefully when she gave me some key pointers.

"Don't hold a judge's gaze," she cautioned. "They want to be looking at you, not the other way around."

"Ah!" I remembered the fact that she'd once been very much an object for boys to look at, when her breast had flopped out of her track suit at that meet in Licking. She knew what it was like to be scrutinized!

"And when you come out on the stage, don't walk directly toward one of the judges. That's too forceful. Point yourself a little to one side or the other."

"OK." Of course, she was being pretty forceful herself right here, giving me clear directions about how to proceed. She was a talented musician, but also a strong person.

"And one last thing." But then she hesitated, giving me a questioning look.

"Yes?"

She glanced around to be sure no one else was too close to us. She smiled and kind of ducked her head. "I'm not sure I should tell you this," she said. "After all, you're older."

"Well, yes, but you've done this before. And you've played so many concerts, when I'm really performing in public for the first time."

"Yeah, but this is about experience in other areas, and I don't know what you've . . . if you've . . . oh, hell, here goes!"

Whoa! Liz used strong language, too! I decided this was slumber party talk, and, since I'd never been to this kind of event with a lot of girls, I shouldn't be surprised. The only sleepovers I'd had were with Sandy, just the two of us.

"Now you know what those judges are thinking when you play the flute, don't you?" Even in the dim light, I could see a twinkle in her eye.

"They're listening to the music?" I really didn't have a clue what she was suggesting.

"They're watching your hands. . . ." She paused, leaned closer to me, and lowered her voice to a whisper.

"And your lips. . . ."

"My lips. . . ."

"And they're thinking. . . ." I could barely hear her now. Leaning closer, I put my ear almost to her lips. "They're thinking of what it would be like if you were playing them!"

She paused, then added one final instruction. "Be sure to let them think you'd like to!"

It took a moment for the image in my head to transform itself, from a flute to a mouth organ. But there it was. I was back where Randy had wanted me to be months before! Could this be so?

Then I thought of Mr. Pierce and decided that it could.

8

I think I probably got about three hours of sleep on the night of Sally's slumber party. But, when you're young, that's plenty for the next day, especially if you believe you're coming up on a life-changing event.

Oh, I think I snuck a short nap in there somewhere, probably late morning. And, even though I was supposed to be practicing my music later, some parts of that afternoon were surely spent resting. This all occurred long enough ago that I don't remember all the details.

True, the big events of that year in my life stick out in my memory even now. But there are also some gaps, even on crucial days, where I can't recall what I was doing or even, in some cases, where I was.

The major events followed one another in a pattern that seemed almost inevitable at the time: buying a flute, having a concert, deciding to enter the pageant; practices, the competition itself, and the final result. Of course, now I see another pattern hidden beneath this apparently seamless chain, one thing following another along a buried sequence of causality. And when I review it all from the perspective of several decades later, I find a finished cycle that may satisfy my desire for order even as it frustrates my sense of justice.

One place I do remember being on the day of the competition is Fanny's Dairy Delite. I'd come by there in the middle of that Saturday afternoon, probably taking our usual cruising route through town, to make sure my best friend was going to be out in the audience for me.

As I pulled into the lot at Fanny's, I studied for a moment the structure of Mrs. Hamilton's and Miss Powers' building. It looked kind of like a miniature airplane hangar, with vertical side walls and an arching metal roof.

I knew that it had originally been a small warehouse for the shoe factory in Fairfield. They made Buster Brown shoes. Packing supplies had been stored here until the shoe business outgrew both factory and warehouse. As they negotiated with the town for incentives to construct a larger plant in a location just south of town, the company's main office abruptly decided to move the entire operation to South Carolina.

"Of course, I'll be there," Sandy told me, almost insulted. "I'm going to see you wear the crown." She was at the counter, but there were no other customers, so she could talk with me.

Fanny's had the standard "Order Here" and "Pick Up Here" positions at the counter. At one point, these had been windows in a front wall of the building, and customers stood in a little enclosed porch. But the business had done well enough that the owners later added an entire front room with booths and tables. The windows and the surrounding section of wall were removed.

"Well, I don't know about receiving the crown," I said to Sandy.

"Blind Bill Martin said you might win." I stirred the Coke I'd bought with a straw and looked back at the empty customer area. As I think about it now, the lack of business probably meant I was there in the middle of the afternoon.

"Bill Martin did? When was that?"

"He was in here a few days ago. Talked about how nice you were." Uh-oh, this sounded like I was still "sweet." But Sandy went on, "And you play the flute really well, he said."

"My mom thinks I've come a long way, and that I should keep playing even after the pageant. I guess I will."

The realization that I wanted to continue playing had come to me more than once recently. I'd found considerable satisfaction in working on my solo, Nelhybel's "Passacaglia." Although it wasn't the only thing I played every day, I'd taken about six weeks to really perfect my performance.

My mom insisted I still play regular exercises to warm up, and she kept finding old pieces she'd learned years ago for me to attempt. At the end of each session, I'd practice the solo, concentrating on a particular section each time. In the last few weeks, even I could see how I'd gone from mechanically playing each note to feeling and expressing the music, the underlying idea that gave life to the whole.

At Fanny's, I had to step away from the counter for a mother and her two children, who were out for ice cream even on a cold day. I overheard her explain to Sandy that her daughters were going to share a banana split to celebrate good six-week report cards from second and fourth grades. I wandered back to a corner booth, where I could watch what was going on but also think through some of my own concerns.

My mom, by the way, was still playing the flute, too. It wasn't just that Tricia was away at school and I generally took care of myself, giving her more time in her housekeeping routine. She'd deliberately dedicated a portion of her day to music. She claimed this was just so she could keep instructing me, but I'd realized pretty quickly that the return of her own skills gave her special pleasure.

Watching Sandy build those banana splits made me realize she, too, was enjoying what she did. She had a bounce to her step as she moved around the kitchen area, and there was flair in her pouring, dipping, and sprinkling.

Using soft ice cream, Sandy had to work faster than she would have with the traditional stuff. She didn't want the three scoops along the length of the banana to melt before they were well covered with strawberry sauce, hot chocolate, and caramel and the whole was topped by whipped cream, chopped nuts, and the traditional maraschino cherries.

Sandy was a whiz at peeling and slicing the banana for a banana split. She capped it with a swift slice of the paring knife, then slit the whole lengthwise while its skin was still on. After prying it open with her hands inserted along the cut, she flipped it over and bent back the peel so that the clean fruit fell in two pieces into the dish below.

"Say, Sandy," I said when she was done with the lady's order. She was due for a break and had slid into the booth with me. "You know, not long ago I asked you about Mr. Pierce?"

"You did?"

I thought back. "Well, I tried to. But you ended up telling me the history of soft ice cream."

"Yeah. It's neat, isn't it?"

"OK, but some of the girls have said some things about him, about. . . ."

"Now that you mention it, I did hear something . . . . odd."

"Oh?"

"Actually, Miss Powers said some of the teachers she knew had been talking about him. I overheard her telling this to Flora."

"What was the question?"

"Well, one of the teachers thought she saw Mr. Pierce at the Banner Hotel."

"A lot of people go there to eat. I hear it's got a good restaurant."

The Banner, of course, was the big Route 66 establishment in Fairfield. I had to learn its history for the Miss Route 66 Pageant.

A grand construction, especially for this relatively remote community, it had been built in the 1930s to host the more prosperous travelers sightseeing along

Route 66. The Banner became a major stop between St. Louis on the eastern edge of the state and Tulsa, Oklahoma.

Meriwether Clark, a successful St. Louis automobile dealer, purchased fifty acres and put up the luxury hotel along the Ozark ridge that bordered one side of Fairfield. The rooms were large, the furnishings elegant, the service first-class.

Fanny's Dairy Delite was a much more modest roadside attraction, though it was probably more popular with locals. And it had a very busy summer season.

Sandy continued with her gossip about Mr. Pierce. "The teacher thought she saw him there with someone, not his wife."

"Not Mrs. Pierce?"

"She was smaller and younger. Or so the woman thought. Smaller and younger and prettier. Weird, huh?"

9

Well, it wasn't so weird if you'd seen Mr. Pierce lean over a booth at Fanny's and drool at you. Or if you'd heard wise Mary's hints that he was someone to watch out for.

So I was getting more and more reason to keep my distance from Fairfield High's assistant principal, even as events were drawing me closer and closer to him. We would meet that night at the college auditorium, the night of the pageant competition. And I would hear from him even before then.

As I was getting ready to say good-bye to Sandy at Fanny's and go home to dress, who should drop in but my mother?

"Mom! What are you doing here?"

"I might be looking for you! Shouldn't you be at home getting your things together?"

"I was just leaving. Um, how did you get here?" I had been driving the Rambler, and it was unusual for her to take our big car, a Ford Galaxy.

"I've got the Ford. Your Dad went with Mr. Robinson to play golf. And I had several errands to run."

Golf? There was another surprise! True, my Dad had told me about his days on a course close to his base in England, back in the war. But the day he'd swung a club out by the bomb shelter was the closest he'd come to actually playing since those days.

Then Miss Powers came up to my Mom. "Hi, Margaret. Glad you could stop by." She opened the little door in the counter by which workers passed through into the kitchen area.

"I'll see you at home soon, Susan," said my mother. They disappeared behind the ice cream machines.

Now what in the world was going on here, I wondered. I didn't even know my mother was friends with Miss Powers. Nor could I think what project or interest they shared that would lead to their meeting here.

Of course, my mother did have a life of her own. I didn't really witness her daytime activities while I was off at school, so who knew how she filled her day?

For years, when Tricia and I were younger, she had worked hard at housekeeping--laundry, cooking, cleaning. But over time those chores had become less time-consuming, both because we were older and did our share, but also because new household appliances saved time and labor.

I wish, by the way, I'd kept a record of the dates such new products entered our home: the washer with the wash-rinse spin-dry cycles replacing the old wringer model; the stovetop pressure cooker that shortened the preparation time for many dishes; the dishwasher that attached to the faucet at the kitchen sink, which, though cumbersome to move in and out of place, still reduced the effort of cleaning up.

I ought to have kept a neat chronology tracing the fulfillment of a dream for the homemakers of

182

Thomas Edison and Alexander Graham Bell's time. A much more efficient kitchen was beginning to emerge in those days of invention and refinement. Women who had had literally to labor in the home began to manage machines which did their work. And that allowed different skills to emerge, new kinds of wives and mothers to appear.

There were those, I know, who turned most of their newly acquired free time to leisure: in my Mom's generation, more morning radio soap operas; expanded sessions of over-the-fence afternoon gossip; additional episodes of "I Love Lucy" and "The Ed Sullivan Show" in the evenings. But my mother, I would gradually learn, turned her energy to other projects.

As I drove home in the Rambler, completing the teenagers' regular route across town, I played back a mental picture of my mother coming into Fanny's, greeting me, retreating with Miss Powers. She was slender, fast-moving, purposeful.

Of course, these thoughts of others faded as I neared home and my challenges for the rest of the day: getting ready, competing, avoiding Mr. Pierce. Two things gave me some confidence at least: the company I was keeping, and the attention of Larry Thornton.

I know, I'd not found Larry and his earnestness and his science projects terribly compelling thus far in life. He was not part of the glamour, attention, and recognition I thought I might get out of the Miss Route 66 competition, even if I didn't win.

His brother Paul was older, bigger, and better-looking. He also resided in that more sophisticated world of college, a sphere above and beyond those mundane realms of childhood--neighborhood and high school. So I'd let my fantasies revolve around the elder Thornton.

But I'd also found myself thinking about Larry lately, how he'd come over to the Circle several times to talk with me. At first I'd thought he was visiting Billy and Mark, but gradually I realized that this was a pretext for seeing me. He'd been pleasant and interesting as he considered the pears in our neighborhood, the remnants of an old orchard. Maybe my understanding of him was maturing just as our local fruit always moved from blossom to fruit to harvest.

He did seem to have a sense of humor, or at least a capacity for sly amusement, underneath his steady application. And those worms of his, the idea of a worm farm. I'd begun to come around a bit in appreciation of those earth movers, compost makers, soil generators. When you thought about it, the world needed worms.

Too, worms had sex. Ever since last summer and Randy's "mouth organ" campaign, I had been struggling with how far to go with this sex business. Although it was slimy and entangling, even worm sex could be appreciated, according to Larry. You just had to see it as a natural feature of the animal kingdom.

I'd loved kissing and cuddling and petting with Randy (when he'd stop there!). But conventional morality restricted my full enjoyment of those events

184

as preludes to a forbidden act. It also seemed possible I could be hurt by that hard lump in Randy's jeans. So I'd turned to a gentler lover, myself.

And now Larry had asked me out. He was more appealing than Randy had been. Even if he wasn't his brother, wouldn't he likely grow to be more like Paul as we finished high school and went on to college?

And then there were these new friends of mine, the other contestants for the title of Miss Route 66. I'd gone into the pageant to assert a me who was not just "sweet." But I found that I liked Elizabeth Rogers, whose piano playing encouraged me in my music. And Mary Dunkin--who could swim powerfully, give dramatic readings, tell off-color jokes--had treated me as a special pal, filling me in on the dynamics of such events.

Even my chief rival, Sally Winchester, exhibited a confidence, poise, and assertiveness that I admired. The slumber party had shown me another side of her character, too, the graceful loser who wanted others to have a good time. And there were more: Jean Templeton, Shirley Bast, Lynn Masingham, and some whose names I'd have to refer to that yellowed program in my briefcase to recall.

Taller and shorter than I, younger and older, darker and fairer, these fellow aspirants to success came together in a kind of sorority, a sisterhood of lovely and talented young women. And I was one of them.

I thought of the quadrangle through which I walked on the way to rehearsals and where I would pass by that night. Its different buildings surrounding a manicured lawn represented the varied academic disciplines of higher education--the sciences, arts, humanities. It was a balance of views, a combination of strengths that created the university.

I didn't fully understand this structure then, of course, as I was a number of months from my own college career. Now, however, I can appreciate this ancient social construct, as old as the buildings at Oxford and Cambridge.

Were the fifteen girls competing for the Miss Route 66 crown a similar arrangement of strengths and perspectives? They may very well have been. Well, fourteen of them, that is. One girl separated herself from the group. But on the night of the pageant itself the remaining contestants banded together to protect themselves and to preserve something they valued. It was not an easy task, but it may well have made me what I am today.

10

Mr. Pierce called me on the phone later in the afternoon, not long after I'd had my conversation with Sandy.

"Hello?" I'm pretty sure I was alone at the house, my mother not home from Fanny's, my dad still out at the golf course. I would feel pretty alone no matter what.

"Hello, Susan? It's Mr. Pierce. I'm calling about the pageant."

"Oh, Mr. Pierce. Hello, sir. Um, I'm not sure I . . . I don't know if I should, um, talk on the phone on, you know, the day of the competition." I looked around the living room, somehow thinking I'd see the reason I should hang up now.

"Oh, it's OK, Susan. Remember, I'm the Senior Consultant, and it's my job to check up on all the contestants, especially right now, to make sure everything's ready for the big show."

"Well, I'm ready. I've got my outfits, the flute. I'll be there at 6:45, right on time."

You might suspect I was trying to close off this conversation. His voice had the same odd wet sound it had had on the day he made the Coke glass sing at Fanny's Dairy Delite, and I was still thinking of Sandy's recounting of teacher gossip.

"That's good. But, Susan, there's something more I . . . *shhph!* . . . need to tell you about . . . *shhph!* . . .

tonight's performance." In the pauses of his speech I could hear a soft slurping sound, perhaps his tongue running over his lips to gather extra saliva, or a sucking sound, air being drawn in.

It surely occurs to you, friendly reader living so many years after this event, that I could have just hung up the phone at this point, perhaps even banged the receiver onto the base. Just because this man had called didn't mean I had to listen, did it? Unfortunately, it did. In those days it would have been hard for a girl to hang up on any male, man or boy.

If a man called, a young girl would assume he wanted to talk to her father. Or perhaps a tradesman or a repairman would ask to talk to the "lady of the house." In either case, the daughter would request politely for him to wait while she called out for the parent involved.

If neither mother nor father was at home, she'd have to let the caller deliver a message, probably searching around on the phone table for a piece of paper and a pencil to write it down. All this etiquette made it difficult for me to think that I could take control of the situation, that I didn't have to let Mr. Pierce continue until he announced the conversation was over.

Had he been a younger caller, another set of rules would have applied, but they, too, required me to stay on the line. Girls waited for boys to call and ask them for dates in those days. We didn't ever phone boys, of course, to see if they'd go out with us. We could decline an invitation or accept, but we had to listen to the entire request and any related explanation.

So, even though I knew I didn't want to hear what this man had to say, I stood essentially frozen in our downstairs hall with the telephone held to my ear.

"I wonder, Susan, how much do you want to win tonight?"

"Excuse me?"

"The pageant. You do want to be Miss Route 66, don't you?"

"Well, yeah. I mean, that's why I entered."

"That's what I thought. Every girl wants to win a beauty contest. Or at least be a finalist, right?"

I slumped down into a sitting position on the hall rug. My back rested against the wall, and I jacked my knees up to my chest.

"I . . . I'm going to do my best, Mr. Pierce. I know all the girls will."

"Yes, of course. Now, Sally really is the favorite. She was first runner-up last year, and she's got a terrific routine. That little baton of hers climbs all over her body!"

In addition to the many spins, twirls, and tosses of traditional routines, Sally now moved the baton by twisting, arching, stretching her body. It slid across her shoulders, rolled down an arm, bounced off her thigh onto a hip, rested on the upper curve of her backside. All with no hands.

I heard that sucking sound again in the earpiece but didn't say anything. What could I have said?

"So, Susan, I don't know how you could beat Sally, it being your first time in the competition and all. But first runner-up, now that's a possibility. You'd like that, wouldn't you?"

I wrapped part of the phone cord around my finger and stared at the wall opposite to me.

"I . . . I'm just going to do the best I can."

"Have you ever . . . *shhph!* . . . eaten a dreamsicle?"

"What?"

"A dreamsicle. It's kind of a cross between a fudgesicle and popsicle, but different flavors, one on the outside and one . . . *shhph!* . . . inside."

A picture appeared in my mind: the single shape on a stick--like a fudgesicle or Eskimo bar--but not chocolate. It was fruit-flavored with a pale core. (I would later learn it's orange sherbet over vanilla ice cream.)

"Sure. They're very good."

I heard a licking sound on the line again.

"I'm eating one right now, Susan. It's delicious. It's the cream inside that's so good, don't you think?"

"Mr. Pierce . . . I, uh, I think I have to get ready. Don't you have to get ready?"

"A lot of people are put off by the idea of a dreamsicle, the flesh-colored outside. They don't realize how good the cream inside is. You just lick enough . . . *shhph!* . . . to get the good stuff to come out."

Somewhere along here I began to feel flushed, queasy, almost sick to my stomach. All sorts of bits and pieces of information were coming together into a complete picture, a finished scenario. I thought of Randy's frustration on dates, remembered Larry's worms suddenly exposed to light, pictured Paul's rigid, hip-riding slide rule.

"Anyway," continued Mr. Pierce, with suddenly more energy. "Here's what I think we can do. I know the judges; I've worked with them for some years now. They're good guys. They'll listen to suggestions. Suppose I '*suggest*' they pay special attention to the flute player, the one with the . . . umm . . . nice flat . . . *shhph!* . . . tummy."

I heard the wet sound again.

"Aren't they going to pay attention to all of the girls?" I asked tentatively. "We all have to perform and wear the outfits."

"Yes, of course, but they'll listen to me; they'll know I'm making a sort of recommendation. You know, I've recommended the last three winners of the pageant, the last three Misses Route 66, and two runners-up."

"Really?"

"A fact. Of course, I'd . . . want you to do me a favor, a little favor, if I recommended you."

"Have you recommended that they pay special attention to Sally?"

"Hmm? Well, what I'm talking about here is first runner up, Susan, a great honor. Why, if anything happens to Sa . . . to the winner, you could be Miss Route 66!"

"I see."

"What I'm going to do, Susan. What I'm going to do is, I'm going to figure you understand what I'm saying. And later this evening, when Bill Martin is keeping the crowd happy while the girls are changing for your final appearance. . . ."

"The swimsuit competition?"

"Right. The judges will be comparing their scorecards and thinking about who should be the finalists. I want you to slip over to where I'm at. I'll be in that little changing room by the back right stage entrance. You know the one?"

"Yes."

"You come on in there for just a few minutes. And, after that, I'll talk to the judges."

"After . . . after what?"

"After you . . . *shhph!* . . . try a . . . dreamsicle."

Volume Four: Harmony. Chapter 1

As I drove our 1960s Rambler American out of the driveway in the Circle that fateful night, I would have liked nothing more than to pick up Sandy and cruise the town of Fairfield, as if I had no cares in the world. No task to perform, challenge to meet, goal to reach. No dirty old man waiting for me in the dressing room by the back stage entrance of the auditorium.

I would have taken Highway 00 north to Sixth Street; Sixth east up to Main Street (and downtown); followed Main north to Business Route 66 (also called Kingshighway), which would swing west for a long block, then turn south down to Sixth Street again. It was a circuit teenagers from all over Fairfield and Phipps County took many times in the course of a Saturday night.

That unvarying trip embodied the comfort of the familiar, although I didn't fully understand at the time how important that was. Most of us had been born and raised in Fairfield, so we repeatedly saw the same familiar landmarks, the unchanging touchstones of past and present events: Phipps Lumber Company, the three downtown drugstores (Dixon's, Rexall's, Ninth Street), the southern edge of the college campus, Fanny's Dairy Delite, The DC (a 24-hour truckers' stop).

A lot of my friends fretted about our circular route, claiming to be trapped, caged, circumscribed by the limitations of small-town life. But more of them would later come to understand that the pieces of our world, visible out our car windows, offered a necessary stability, at least for us. We were especially reassured by the institution of family, because just about every rider in the car passed his or her own neighborhood (or the road going into it) on each circuit. And, even though we had to rebel in some ways against their control, we knew where the parents, siblings, grandparents were waiting and watching.

Things are more fragile today, I think--families, neighborhoods, communities. It's a price of success, our nation's prosperity and technology's grand achievements. We're more an urban nation and a people organized by telephones, computers, global financial networks. But I think individual people live more isolated lives now, straining across longer distances to connect in more fragile relationships.

On that night many years ago, I needed the reassurance of the familiar, the stable, the friendly. And in the end, they were all there for me. But they reasserted themselves only after a series of startling shocks to my sense of self and of the world around me.

I will get to take the old cruising route of my home town later today, of course, now that I'm back for this celebration of Fairfield's history. I'll be driving not to the college auditorium, where the Miss Route 66 contest was held years ago, but to the new high school, where wearers of that crown will

194

meet in a kind of reunion. And oh! don't the memories come rushing back as I drink coffee in my room at the Holiday Inn, which sits at the westernmost exit off the freeway, right where old (now "historic") Route 66 disappears into the Interstate.

When I drive east back toward the high school in a few hours I'll have to avoid regressing to my high school self, the young Susan Bell nervously pulling into the college parking lot behind the auditorium, gathering her flute, her outfits, her courage to compete for the crown of Miss Route 66.

I knew that night I'd come a long way since the previous summer, when with Sandy Johnson I first saw a flute for sale in Martin's Jewelry Store. I had learned to play, found family support to become a contestant, made new friends like Mary Dunkin and Elizabeth Rogers. But tonight was my biggest test.

"Good luck!" said a voice as I climbed the stairs to the room where all the girls would spread out their clothes and equipment.

"Oh, Larry! Ah, thanks." My classmate and soon-to-be date had arrived behind me and now was turning down the first floor hall to the entrance for auditorium seating.

"You'll do great," he offered, smiling, and then went on.

As I watched him stride away, I suddenly thought, is he taller? He looks bigger, more filled out, too. But perhaps it's just the sports jacket and dress slacks, a change from his everyday school self (or weekend worm farmer self!). I wondered if I'd look good to him in my swimsuit.

Larry's voice was also reassuring in its gentleness, in the straightforward nature of his encouragement. Of course, mentally, I was comparing it to Mr. Pierce's sleazy invitation on the telephone of only a few hours earlier.

There were other friendly voices echoing inside my head as I approached this great test of my ambition. My mother's encouragement came not only in words, but in music. At times in the last few weeks she'd spoken sharply about my playing, insisting that I practice key measures at a slower pace, play others loudly that I would eventually sound softly, measure the changes in tempo against the metronome. But always she praised the final result.

In my mind, though, I heard, alongside her words of instruction, notes from her flute. "Do-re-mi-fa-sol-la-ti-do," that flute had sung many months ago. And, recovering her own music from early years of training, she'd gone on to fill our home with polished melodies, played primarily for her own pleasure but certainly creating a new sense of richness for my father and me.

My dad's voice, too, sounded in my mind, though more as background, a soft bass over which higher voices carried. I heard him explaining his wartime golfing, the tension and relief of that momentous time.

More distant was the voice with which I'd learned he had courted my mother. He was the telephone engineer who'd rigged up a fancy walkie-talkie and sent his marriage proposal down the line to a young musician. He had called and she had answered.

There was still another voice following me into the auditorium, that of my older sister Tricia. All through my growing up, I had heard her perform at public functions, demonstrating her talent, a certain star quality. I think I'd blotted out that voice during the recent weeks of competition, not wanting to battle her reputation as well as candidates my own age. Tonight, a friend was supposed to be driving Tricia up from Springfield to join my small group of supporters. (To this point I'd heard only the voice of her pet parrot, Juliet.)

I was among the last to arrive in our group dressing room, a regular classroom for the college's theater classes.

"Susan, here's a spot," said Mary. She had saved me a student desk and some space on a portable metal clothes rack. Half a dozen such racks had been set up for the girls, most of whom already were in the required evening gown for the first round of competition. Some mothers, friends, and cousins were busy putting final touches on hair, makeup, the dress itself. I'd told my mom I'd be calmer with her in the audience.

"Do you need some help?" asked Liz Rogers, our runner with great, long legs.

"I'm fine, I think."

I had come dressed in the evening gown, preferring to risk getting it wrinkled on the way there to dressing in front of so many others. I propped my case in the chair of the desk, unpacked and assembled my flute, took a deep breath.

"I think," I said to Liz, "I think I need to just walk about a bit to settle my nerves."

She smiled and patted my shoulder. "Go. Relax. We still have thirty minutes."

After two turns up and down the hall, I slipped for a minute into the area immediately back of the stage. The stage, decorated as the Garden of Eden, was quiet behind the curtain, but I could hear a low murmur from the crowd on the other side. Stepping through a gap in the set's backdrop--the bushes, flowers, and grasses of Paradise--I saw Sally Winchester walking away from the little dressing room where Mr. Pierce had told me to meet him.

The door to that room was closed, so I didn't know if Sally had come from there. And there was no evidence that anyone--say, Mr. Pierce--remained inside.

Frozen in place, I could see that Sally was smiling broadly and that there was even more bounce to her walk than usual.

2

"What are you doing, wandering around the halls?" said a friendly voice beside me.

"Me?" I asked, turning to find Blind Bill Martin cocking an ear in my direction. He was coming from in front of the curtain, probably having just made last-minute checks on his microphone, the podium where he stood, the headset by which he could receive directions from the college's technician who worked the lights.

"Yes, you, Susan, the flute player," he said, smiling. Could he tell it was me by the sound of my walk, the smell (slight) of my perfume, the elimination of other possibilities? I had no idea.

"I . . . uh," I stammered, watching the retreating back of Sally over Blind Bill Martin's shoulder as she marched toward our common dressing room. "I was just trying to calm my nerves." I adjusted my flute's mouthpiece and tried a few notes.

"Um-hm. Sit with me a minute, young lady." He took my arm at the elbow (how did he know where it was?) and sat us both down on a bench beside the stage's side entrance.

"I'm going to tell you the story of my first record contract. You do want to hear it, don't you?"

His manner was fatherly and gentle--but insistent. So, of course, I prepared myself to listen.

I would come to wonder some time later if Blind Bill Martin knew that Sally had just passed him in the hall, if he suspected where Mr. Pierce was right then (in the little dressing room, as I had guessed myself), if he, Tiresias-like, could tell what it was like to be a man and what it was like to be a woman. Whatever he knew at that moment, the brief story he told me that evening contained kernels of wisdom I have never forgotten.

"I grew up on a farm outside Calico Rock, Arkansas, down on the White River," he said. I nodded as if I knew where that was. Some months later I would find it on a map not far south of the Missouri border. And then years after that, on a trip to Memphis, I would take a detour through this hamlet to see the region where the Martins came from. It's remote even for the Ozarks.

"My daddy and his daddy," Blind Bill went on, "and a bunch of cousins, they were musicians. Good ones, too."

"I see." I was continuing to blow softly into my flute, keeping it warm and trying to calm myself.

"Hello there, Mary," Blind Bill said. My fellow contestant was passing us on her way to a rest room.

"Hi, Blind Bill," Mary said brightly. "Blind Bill" was my friend's stage name, by the way, and he had insisted from the beginning of rehearsals that all the girls call him that. "Big crowd, Susan," she said to me.

I squirmed on the bench, thinking of all those townspeople waiting to criticize my clothes, my walk, my flute playing.

200

"I was born blind, you know, so I never missed seeing. And I could strum on Daddy's guitar when I wasn't four years old. Sing anything I'd ever heard."

"I only started playing the flute last summer."

"You told me that, and you've learned fast. You may have real talent. 'Course that's what they all told me from my childhood on up. 'You got a gift, Blind Bill.' 'You gonna be on the radio.' 'You'll be going far one day, you Blind Bill.'"

"I guess they were right," I agreed, but I secretly didn't think Fairfield was all that far from Calico Rock.

"I been to Nashville, you know?"

"Is that right?"

"Sure. Sang at the Opry, met some famous people there. But that's not what I want to tell you about tonight."

"Oh?" I was beginning to get nervous, looking around for a clock to make sure I wasn't going to be late for the pageant's beginning, that moment when the curtain rose on all of us standing at the back of the stage. But Blind Bill, it turned out, knew time along with everything else.

"You relax now, quit squirming. We've got a few more minutes before all that business in there gets started."

"OK. But it's not just the show. . . ."

"I know that too, honey. Now, you just listen. I remember the first agent to come down our way, a Kansas City guy, name of Stryker, never forget him.

He heard me play at the county fair over in Mountain Home, I believe it was. I was with a group there headed up by my cousin, Frankie. We were doing old time country tunes, Jimmie Rodgers and the Carter family. I did some singing too, I do believe."

"Um-hm."

"Some of my own songs. I didn't write 'em out, of course. But the group played along with me. I did three, maybe four nice songs I'd been working up. Best was 'Can't See My Mama Now.' You've heard me do that, haven't you?"

"Well, I might have." I suspected he'd been singing that now and then during rehearsals. It wasn't, so far as I knew, one of the songs he would play that night. "Yes, I have."

"Now, Stryker, he took me aside, out in the night air. Gave me a cigarette, offered me a drink. I didn't drink then, and I don't now." He huffed his sense of affront. "And don't you either."

"Oh, I don't. I won't."

"There's temptations, you see. People say they'll do things for you. Ask you to do them favors first."

"Hm-um."

"Stryker, now, he had a contract in his jacket pocket. I heard him take it out, unfold it on the fender of his car. 'I'm going to give you a $100 bill right now, Blind Bill,' he told me. And I heard him snap that new print paper money. That would have meant something like a car in those days. 'And I want you to sign this contract.'"

"So you'd have a deal, then, with a recording company?"

"That's the way it was supposed to be. He said, 'I got this pen, Blind Bill. It's from the president of my company.' And he put it in my hand, wanting me to feel the size of it. It was a big, fat one, heavy too."

"The official company contract-signing pen," I agreed. I wondered if someone, the mayor, would sign a proclamation that I was the next Miss Route 66 with such a pen.

"'Then,' says Stryker, 'then, you'll get royalties on every song you record. We'll make sure they get played on the radio all across the country. You'll be a rich man. They'll ask you to come sing your hits-- Kansas City, Omaha, St. Louis.'"

"It sounds like it was a good deal, Blind Bill. I mean, if it was like he said. If it was a genuine contract and all."

"Um-hm. You're right to say that, Susan. If it was all written down the way he said. 'Course I couldn't read it. You know that; I knew that; and that Stryker knew that."

"And it wasn't the way he said it was?"

"No, it wasn't."

"So you didn't sign?"

"Oh, I signed all right. Took that big pen he'd put in my hand; let him put my hand there on the paper right where he wanted it; and put down a right fine signature. 'Course I signed 'John Hancock' for him." He laughed. "He didn't even look."

"He was trying to trick you, and you tricked him!"

"That's right. He went off thinking he'd fooled this ignorant hillbilly. But I knew how these deals work. You think you're signing with the company and that they'll get you jobs and sell your records. But if your songs don't sell, they drop you but won't let you sign with anyone else. If your songs do sell, you still don't make the big money. The company does."

"You mean you're stuck with the deal you didn't understand?"

"That's right. You find you've given away something you didn't intend to, your freedom, your future."

"I see." I was beginning to think Blind Bill understood a lot about more things than the recording business.

"Hey, young lady, it's time for the show to begin. This could be your moment."

"I don't know. I don't feel much like Miss Route 66 yet."

"You just be Susan Bell. That's good enough for anybody."

And, I'm pleased to say, that's just what I did.

3

In retrospect, I've decided that the evening gown competition is the right place to begin a beauty contest. The girls are uniformly presented in the traditional format of bare shoulders, tight waist, and full dresses. So there's only so much one can do to stand out other than trust your figure.

There's also a neatness in this event: announcement of contestants (a beginning); parade across the stage (middle); resumption of the group order (an ending). Such cycles, as I've told you, always appeal to me. In the case of this process, of course, as in so many others, there was more than one thread connecting the parts together and leading to a conclusion.

For beginners in such competition, like me, staying composed within poses already established by contest rules is comforting. And that was what I wanted right then: simply to survive my first public appearance under the lights, on the stage, before the crowd. I counted on my slim waist at the center of that outfit.

Veterans of the evening gown event, on the other hand, knew other ways to draw attention to themselves even within this constricting situation. Sally Winchester, for one, began a distinctive pursuit of the crown even when encased in the same dress the rest of us were wearing.

I learned this only later, as, concentrating simply on not shaking and not falling, I didn't at the time observe much going on around me. Well, I did carry on an intermittent, whispered, stiff-lipped conversation with Liz, who stood next to me.

"You nervous?" she whispered while others were still taking their places. The curtain had not gone up.

"You bet!"

Mr. Pierce had arranged us in a semicircle at the back of the stage, tallest girls in the center and shorter ones down the line toward stages left and right. The small orchestra was playing the inevitable theme song for such events, "There she is, Miss America. . . ." (We were supposed to think "Miss Roo-oute Sixty-six".) When the curtain went up, Blind Bill introduced us as a group, then called us forward one by one.

We didn't do the famous walk out toward the judges and back right away, but simply stepped forward and waved to the crowd as our names were called. When all contestants were back in the row, Blind Bill explained the criteria the judges were using to rank us in the evening gown competition: stance, walk, turn, and return.

Since all three judges were men, I now know there were other, probably more telling criteria: bust, especially as revealed and in motion above the gown's top; hip pivot as we advanced; rump action in reverse. Oh, I suppose our faces counted some, too. With stage makeup, though, we all looked remarkably alike.

When he had introduced us, Blind Bill described the dress we were all wearing. He explained that Mr. Simpson, our well-known local merchant, had made these dresses available to contestants. And the way he said it suggested that Mr. Simpson was a civic-minded sponsor, sacrificing profit to support the town event. But, as you know, we'd each had to pay full price for the outfit.

Then began the parade of contestants, each of us walking to the front of the stage, looking left and right, then crossing from one side to the other before returning to our original places. I was among the first girls to go and, I suppose, passed this initial test with adequate scores. When I resumed my place in the line, Liz made me aware of Mr. Pierce off-stage to my right.

"You see him?" Liz whispered.

"You mean Mr. Pierce? What about him?"

"Yes. He's turning red!"

I snuck a peek to the side and saw what she meant. His face was flushed and his eyes glaring.

I had assumed at first that he would simply be watching the proceedings, anticipating perhaps the changes that would have to be made for the talent phase that came next--moving the piano, clearing space for baton twirling, setting up the podium used in dramatic readings. Instead he was intensely interested in something on stage.

The other girls took their walk, all of us continuing to look about the same to me. The thin ones wore the gown loosely, so their bony figures weren't conspicuous. Some bulges on heavier girls were smoothed by the tight fit the waist.

Liz Rogers, whose breast had famously flopped out in a track meet, did score well in this event. She wasn't that big, but what she had rose and fell provocatively as she walked. I watched her bosom sink and swell as she strode confidently away from the stage front. Alas, there had been no jiggle on my chest.

Finally Sally took her walk. How did she get to be last? This was clearly the best position for a strong candidate, leaving a lasting final image in the judges' minds. The first person is easily forgotten by the end. And as anyone knows who's watched Olympics judges rank figure skaters, each person after the first--who doesn't fall--tends to get a higher ranking.

Sally let the applause for the girl before her subside to near silence. Smiling broadly, she took her walk. And as she went forward, the rest of us on stage--and surely the judges--noticed something peculiar: a steady, rushing, swishing sound.

"What's that?" whispered Liz beside me, so softly I could still hear the sound coming from Sally.

"I don't know . . . unless. . . ."

"It's coming from her, from that girl."

"Yes, it's . . . it's her legs."

I can't imagine what kind of long distance bill she had run up in searching, but Sally had gotten (probably through mail order) an early form of panty hose. And that new sheer fabric literally sang as her legs rubbed together. No, it wasn't so much a singing

208

as a humming, a human version of the cricket's mating call.

Sally's humming was present whenever she walked, but it didn't stop immediately when she did, as if some unseen movement under the dress continued. And it was powerfully erotic, as a quick glance at the faces of Misters Rodd, Pollman, and Systrunk revealed. One, I'm sure, was drooling. The sound recalled the hum Mr. Pierce's finger made on the Coke glass at the Dairy Delite.

"There goes the evening gown competition," whispered Liz.

To avoid looking like I was talking to Liz, I turned to the side and there saw Mr. Pierce again, his face still red. And now I could tell where his gaze was directed: at Blind Bill Martin.

All that stuff I told you earlier about how well they worked together? Well, I guess it was an act, at least on Mr. Pierce's side. He hated the attention Blind Bill got, from the crowd, but also, of course, from the girls. And even as the pageant progressed, he was hoping for some way to strike at a rival.

Many weeks later I heard Blind Bill on the radio, singing his favorite tunes. I wrote down the words to that song he'd told me about, and they've stayed in my mind ever since. I didn't really believe they applied to Blind Bill himself, of course. I saw them as Mr. Pierce's theme song:

My Mama loved her little boy,

She watched him grow with joy.

But then a man, I rambled and I roamed.

I played too hard, did things I shouldn't have done.

My Mama cried and sorrowed once I'd gone.

Can't see my Mama now, you know,

Can't see my Mama now.

She's up in heaven, an angel pure;

I'm goin' to hell for sure.

My Mama came to see her son,

She visited him in prison.

I shot a man, a drunken brawl'd begun.

He stole my girl, but I shouldn't have used a gun.

My Mamma cried and sorrowed once she'd gone.

Can't see my Mama now, you know,

Can't see my Mama now.

She's up in heaven, an angel pure;

I'm going to hell for sure.

4

It amuses me to think of the variety of talents we potential Misses Route 66 demonstrated that evening long ago: baton twirling, flute playing, bowling pin juggling, archery, tumbling (which was what we called gymnastics then), singing, doing arithmetic in your head, and other skills I can't even recall. What an odd collection of talents!

Still, as I remember that night, I feel that our disparate abilities merged into a single entity, a collection of young aspirations that complemented rather than clashed with each other. I suppose it's too grand to say that we represented the variety of America's female youth, the nation's girlhood in sum. But, now that I think about it again, maybe not.

In the coming years of the tumultuous 1960s and the troubled early 70s, many of us discovered and used talents we hadn't known we possessed. The women's movement picked up energy from the civil rights campaigns of that era, and an important force in our nation's history gained new energy. It didn't come from outside these same girls who wanted to be beauty queens, but from inside, from powerful desires that formerly had been directed into the odd channels of, say, cheerleading or beauty contests.

So, as I pull up from memory images of Janet Paramore tossing balsa wood bowling pins and Martha Walton drawing her bow at a straw-stuffed bull's eye and Cathy Nunn calculating the number of seats in the auditorium in her head, I think not of trivial accomplishment or misspent energy, but of raw potential waiting for its moment, waiting for a future that did occur.

I was in the middle of the order for the talent phase, as we went roughly from simple to complex in terms of equipment and space required: dramatic reading, flute, and piano preceded archery, tumbling, and baton twirling. All I needed was my music stand set in place in the middle of the stage.

I'd brought a collapsible metal stand from home, even though there were others available at the college. I just felt I'd be more comfortable with the same stand I'd used since I began playing.

My stand's three legs--each about eighteen inches long--unfolded at the bottom of the main stem to form a tripod base. A long, thin tube rose from that base to the structure that held the music. It opened at the top like a fan, perhaps eighteen inches wide and a foot high.

"Let me help you with that," said a low voice as I tested it behind the stage. Mr. Pierce was standing at my side, his mouth close to my ear.

"Oh!" I'm afraid I jumped. "Oh, this isn't hard. I do it all the time by myself."

Nevertheless, he pulled the stand from me. Putting both hands on the middle stem, he pushed it down on the floor, spreading the legs and, I guess, testing their firmness.

"This part looks good; the legs spread well," he observed. I noticed that his face was less red now, though there was still a flush to his cheeks and, I thought, a bit of a wild look in his eyes.

"It's fine, really." I tried to take the stand back from him, but he pulled it out of reach, turning his body ninety degrees away from me. He unfolded the top part that held the music, then squeezed it shut again.

"Now, the part that holds the music is functional. Give me what you're playing."

"No, it's OK. I've tested it; it works."

Still holding the stand like a long-necked bird, he kept it at arm's length. But he leaned over toward me and whispered. "The dressing room, back there." He gestured, but I already knew the place he was pointing to. I'd seen Sally come from there earlier.

"Dressing room?" I tried to play dumb. All I wanted right now was the music stand back. "I'm next. Please give me. . . ."

"I'll kiss your flute," he hissed, touching his lips to the folded top section of my music stand. "And you can kiss mine!"

"And now Susan Bell on the flute," called Blind Bill Martin from the front of the stage. Whew! He'd rescued me.

"I'm . . . it's me," I said, reaching for the stand in a frantic, eager way.

At last he let me take it. I guess his desire to keep his position with the pageant remained a strong force in Mr. Pierce: the show had to go on. But I knew I would have to say or do something about his unofficial demand before the swimsuit competition.

Meanwhile, I played the flute. And, you know, nothing makes me prouder now about my role in the entire pageant than the fact that, after yet another unpleasant exchange with the Senior Consultant, I could breathe evenly enough to make music.

I would learn, in fact, that I scored fairly high in the talent competition. My piece was not that ambitious, but I played without flaws and with (according to my mother) attention to the music's subtlety.

Two tangential things, I think, also contributed to the judges' response: they'd not heard a flute solo in any past pageants; and my slender form in the evening gown was accentuated in the effort of playing.

Like Liz, who played the piano, I hadn't changed outfits for my performance. Mary Dunkin also stayed in her evening gown for her reading from Shakespeare's *Twelfth Night*. Sally, on the other hand, needed more freedom of movement in her baton twirling.

Once again this veteran competitor had a trick up her sleeve. Well, no, not up her sleeve, since her outfit had no sleeves. Her outfit was so skimpy the missing sleeves were hardly noticeable, especially when you consider the things she did with that baton!

My own appearance in the formal gown generated an effect similar to what Randy had so clearly felt back in the summer. I was standing up tall, holding my instrument parallel to my shoulders, breathing with my abdominal muscles to sustain the column of air creating music. The standard pageant dress hugged my midsection, and my uplifted arms directed male eyes to my flat, thin middle. It was an effect that would be magnified when I wore the swimsuit Sandy and I had altered at the last minute.

When Sally performed, of course, she made even more of her feminine form. I had maintained a youthful naiveté about the purpose and results of the talent competition in the Miss Route 66 Pageant. I believed that the three judges would impartially identify the best talent, even if they were swayed by other qualities. Such things as audience expectation, performer showmanship, and flamboyant sex appeal were, I felt, peripheral. But Sally knew the full power of these forces.

There were three elements to her winning performance: sight, sound, and motion. I've already mentioned that her outfit was as skimpy as a swimsuit, showing arms, legs, shoulders. She was wearing the same transparent hose that sang as she moved, though, so throughout her routine an erotic hum rose and fell in the judges' ears. But there was a new sound also, a throaty whistle sometimes in counterpoint to her legs' song, at other times echoing it.

Sally had embedded two whistles in the rubber tips of her baton, and they sounded in its many spins and twists. Revolving on her fingertips or soaring close to the ropes that raised and lowered curtains, the baton became another voice of Sally's desire. Its syncopated, deep-pitched tone blended with the hum of her legs and an audible breathing that grew as her effort increased--short, sharp intakes of air as she stepped, jumped, turned. All these sounds expressed her drive to win, her ambition to dazzle and to hold the judges.

The final manifestation of her performance was motion. America was still in that transition between formal ballroom dancing and less scripted, hip-oriented forms not far from the bump-and-grind routines of a stripper. The attention of popular culture had gone below the waist. So, while Fairfield's mayor, the president of Thompson and Pollman Insurance, and the head of our most prestigious law firm began by watching Sally's baton, their eyes traveled south as she performed, and stayed there. She won the talent portion of the competition.

5

"You're in the top three, I'm sure of it," said Mary as we all filed back to the group dressing room after the talent competition.

"You think so?"

"I was watching the judges' eyes when you played the flute. They like you."

"I was so nervous! I'm afraid to look at them. And how do you do well in the evening gown competition? All you can do is walk, and stand there, and walk."

"Trust me. I can tell these things. I don't mean you're winning. Sally's got them hypnotized. But, with your slim figure, you can do well in the swimsuit. You come up big there and you might be first runner-up!"

This was exciting. I'd either been concentrating so hard on not messing up or being shocked by Sally's tactics that I hadn't really thought about whether I might be doing better than the other girls. The runner-up--that would be fun!

I glanced over at Sally, who was examining her face in a hand-held mirror. She curled her lips and studied the mirror, as if worried that some piece of food had gotten stuck in her teeth. They looked bright and clean to me. She flashed a big smile at her own image, then put the mirror down in order to trade her revealing baton twirling outfit for a revealing swimsuit.

Watching her, I remembered Mr. Pierce and the deal he'd offered me over the phone--second to Sally. I could cinch it by doing him a "little favor." But it was a favor I didn't think I could grant. I'd even rather deal with Randy's "mouth organ" than Mr. Pierce's dreamsicle. Ugh!

Out on stage Blind Bill was entertaining the crowd while we all changed into our swimsuits. He was telling stories from past pageants and singing the usual country songs, about hard-hearted women and down-and-out men.

I tried to imagine the perfect ending to the pageant, to my many months of preparation and planning. But all I saw was that little drop of drool in the corner of Mr. Pierce's mouth.

Putting my flute away in its velvet-lined case, I could at least congratulate myself on a fine performance. I realized the instrument I'd bought on a whim had come to feel a part of me. I thought of my mother and her flute, hidden away in the basement for so many years. Why had she given it up, stopped playing music?

When, with Sandy, I'd first carried this flute home, I had been looking for a new mode of expression, even a different self to express. Any musical potential I might have possessed had been ignored by my parents and teachers, not maliciously but probably because of my older sister's more obvious talents.

Once I'd taken the dramatic step of purchasing the flute, my life changed. Daily practice sessions with my mother bred a new confidence and assertiveness, which carried over into other activities. Before long I separated myself from Randy and began to think of different boys, boys of a different sort.

I was probably aiming too high in Paul Thornton, the college guy. But his younger brother Larry had shown some praiseworthy characteristics. He was intelligent and had a plan for college, for life thereafter. And he was interested in me. In fact, he was here in the auditorium, encouraging me to do my best.

Was Paul Thornton here, too? Hmm, probably so. So far as anyone knew, he was still dating Sally. So he'd be here for her. The Thornton family was divided, then, in allegiances at the pageant. Would it be, as we'd learned in American history class, like the Civil War where "brother fought brother"?

Well, no matter what boy I was dating, I wasn't going to abandon the flute. It would remain a symbol of my strength, really, to the end of my days. Why had my mother put aside her talent when she went to work and when she married my father?

If I thought of my neighborhood pears, Mom's life seemed to contradict a natural process: blossom, fruit, seed, plant, and it all begins again. She had been a bud, rich with promise. In school she'd opened in beauty.

Larry, I suppose, could have used a worm's life cycle to describe the same arrested development, but

219

I hadn't paid quite enough attention to his lectures to identify all the correct stages. The point would be the same: something happened to block her growth.

I didn't want to blame my father, competent telephone repairman in early adulthood, established manager through his middle years. Especially because of the story of his proposal--romantically, on a private line--he didn't appear to me as a villain, someone who demanded his wife concentrate only on his career.

True, that's what she had done, support him in his work and raise his children. But she did these things with good cheer, not as if she were a downtrodden, dispirited spouse.

My mother's decision to stop playing must have come before her courtship then, before she met my father. A scenario occurred to me: competition for a music scholarship to some prestigious institution. Mother knew she had a good chance and practiced for months.

After a long bus journey to--where? Oh, let's say William Jewell, Kansas City. She arrives there for an audition, a chance to win a scholarship that will pay for everything, the basis for a later career.

Her parents, who've endured years of scrimping during the Depression to pay for her lessons, are about to achieve their goal. That talent spotted when their daughter was perhaps four or five years old, whistling a tune along with the Sunday school piano, has been nurtured and protected. Now it will carry her on to a future barely imaginable in the little town of her youth. She's on to Chicago, New York, Vienna.

She wins the scholarship! But then the truth becomes clear: in order to study with the great masters here and abroad she must leave her family behind. There is no room for sentiment in this profession. She must sacrifice for her talent, for the benefit of the world of audiences she can inspire.

So, she turns down the scholarship. Yes, that's it. She retreats from greatness, goes to work as a bank teller to help her parents, who are aging. She meets this telephone lineman, falls in love, marries, has children. Her life has been diverted into the small-time domestic realm I have known, her only real outlet the star quality of her elder daughter.

Now I know it's time to go the little changing room, to make my own decision about the future. Do I need to give up on fame and fortune? Why not risk a little, new Susan Bell, you strong person who has found ambition, who knows desire? And this little thing I'm going to do for Mr. Pierce--how bad can it be? It'll go on for a couple of minutes, and then it'll be time for the show.

Down the hall I pass Sally returning. We are both in our swimsuits. She gives me her usual broad smile and says cheerfully, "One more event to go!"

"Yes," I reply, but at the same time I notice her breasts straining against her suit. They seem larger than ever!

Still, I think, I can be runner-up. I draw my shoulders back, suck in my stomach, and walk across the back of the stage to the little changing room. This will only take a minute, a small price for a big first step.

Pierce is there, the door open halfway as he sits in a straightback chair.

"Ah, you're here," he says with a grin. He glances over my shoulder to see if anyone else is nearby. "Let's talk about, um, the order for the swimsuit competition." He stands and backs against the far wall, leaving room for me to come in.

"I . . . " I begin.

"You don't need a chair," he interrupts excitedly. He picks it up with one hand and sets it outside the room. I step aside to give him space and then hesitate on the threshold. "But you need to be quick if I'm also going to talk to the judges."

He grins, and I see his lips are wet with spit.

"Mr. Pierce," I say. "You're going to have to eat your own dreamsicle."

6

I won the swimsuit competition, but lost the pageant--to Sally Winchester, of course.

That's not even the worst of it. Sally also won the award for being the most helpful contestant during all the preparations, Best Roadside Attraction. Now we all understood the reason for her slumber party the night before and her solicitous concern that the other girls have a good time at her house.

Still, there were things for me to be pleased with. Greatest of all, of course, was the satisfaction I felt at having confronted Pierce. And having rejected his proposition. In the Miss Route 66 Pageant, I would go only as far as my own abilities and looks would take me.

Not that the confrontation with that man in the changing room didn't chill my soul, young and basically innocent person that I was. I feared his interest in me, and I feared his disinterest.

I had always assumed he could use his influence with the judges to hurt as well as help my chances to become Miss Route 66. But he might have been able to pursue me after the pageant as well, using his power as assistant principal at the school. Could he change my schedule, put me in classes I didn't want to take, even keep me from graduating? I didn't know, but I worried.

Still, in the end, I knew I had to take my chances as his enemy, rather than become the kind of friend he wanted. For I sensed that, if I did this thing once for him, he would ask me to repeat it. And repeat it.

Years later I would be able to imagine more concretely what might have happened had I closed the door behind me and the Pageant's Senior Consultant. Well, there was what he hoped would happen, and probably a different scenario in reality.

Don't forget that Sally had been in there with him not more than an hour earlier. Later revelations would confirm that she had been willing to do what he asked (though what actually happened with the two of them was never confirmed by either).

If Sally had succeeded in doing what he wanted, it's unlikely that he would have been ready for a second go-around with me. And if she'd failed, he'd have been less likely with a novice to, shall we say, rise to the occasion.

Oh, why don't I be even more blunt: if Sally had failed, no female in Fairfield would have succeeded. Poor thing, she knew how to satisfy in those situations. But I'm coming to that unseemly part of the story. First, let me narrate the swimsuit competition, where I did so well.

Not only did I impress the judges, but I actually enjoyed this event.

"And now we have the part I like the most," joked Blind Bill at the beginning, as if he could see to rank us. "Our gorgeous contestants will model the latest in swimsuit wear, and our three judges will see who steps the proudest."

This time I was near the end of the procession, so I watched others take their turns around the stage. At some points I even relaxed enough to scan the audience.

"Sporting a traditional one-piece suit that you might see at Sunset Beach or down in Miami, here is Elizabeth Rogers."

I watched Larry watch Liz. He seemed attentive but not excited. How did I want him to see me?

How did Blind Bill remember what we were wearing, where we stood (especially after we'd changed our order for the different events), what he was supposed to say to keep the pageant moving along?

"Mary Dunkin comes next, and her outfit has a patriotic flavor--red, white and blue."

Larry watched her the same way he had Liz, about the way I would have expected him to watch the evening gown competition.

He was sitting, by the way, next to my sister Tricia, I realized. Up until then, I hadn't known if she'd arrived in time, driving up from Springfield. A veteran of many public appearances, she was completely relaxed. My parents were next to her on the other side.

"And in a two-piece suit, the rage on the French Riviera, I'm told--here is Sally Winchester."

I watched Larry carefully here. Would he be mesmerized like all the other boys, like the three male judges? Would his mouth gape open, his eyes light up, his breathing increase?

Hmm. He doesn't change. He looks, he sees, but he is not conquered. I like that. But he'd better look differently at me!

As I think I mentioned, Sandy had recommended a change in the suit I was wearing. It was a standard one-piece, which my mother had insisted on. She wasn't ready for the one I had wanted.

Most of the two-piece suits in those days had high waists, coming right to or above the navel, and they were cut like short shorts at the bottom, showing none of your derriere. The tops were large also, much bigger than the string and cups of future bikinis.

But I'd found one suit with a low-slung bottom half. It was still full in the legs, but it showed two inches below my navel. I pleaded, but my mother vetoed. (Actually, I now agree with her decision.)

Later, Sandy proposed a change in the traditional one-piece we'd finally purchased. Without my mom's knowledge, she cut a large oval out of the middle. It reached from two inches below my breasts to one inch below my bellybutton. The widest portion was above my waist, but that only accentuated the swell of my hips and the smooth plane of my tummy.

A few years later I realized that this cut outlined the shape of my belly when pregnant, at least through most of the time I was carrying. My babies rode high until they were ready to arrive.

Anyway, when I walked out on the stage I surprised the other contestants, the audience, and my parents, to be sure. I turned sideways several times so they could all see how flat my belly was. And I knew my bare navel rode in flesh never before seen in the Miss Route 66 Pageant. I was a hit!

In retrospect, I see the swimsuit competition as the silliest in the pageant. Talent certainly makes sense. And wearing an evening gown well is something women can expect to do in adult life--that is, appear in public in the accepted dress for special occasions. But parade around in a swimsuit? Nothing could be more artificial.

Yes, I know, girls go to the beach and hope to catch the eyes of boys there. But it's really a tease, offering something you don't value for something else you wish to secure.

Magazines and television advertisers love to use the woman in the bikini to sell products. And the contestant showing the judges her figure matches a model displaying the latest attire on the runway of a fashion show. But neither of those occasions presents the individual, only the product she carries.

So the swimsuit competition is really an exercise in fueling male lust. We titillate to arouse but not to satisfy. In a twisted way, Pierce was right to seek completion of the cycle. The rest of the men in that auditorium that night contemplated possessing the objects they saw without commitment to the larger cycle of human interaction it suggests. I mean, of course, some notion of domestic or marital love, the reproduction of the species.

All this is not to say that we weren't proud of what we could show. Mary's swimming had trimmed the shape of her long legs and given her a firm rear end. I knew that when she walked back toward the rest of us her tight bottom had our three town fathers forgetting the heavier forms of their middle-aged wives.

Sally's triumph was all up top, in the breasts that men in that era dreamed about. She jiggled them when she walked, she swung them in turning, she hoisted them in perfect profile with deep breaths and the pull of her shoulders. I even heard one of the girls down the line to my left gasp in admiration.

And me too. I offered up my flat tummy to that gathering. And I wanted them--at least all the males--to like it.

Well, I offered my tummy to everyone but Blind Bill. He didn't see it, and his praise was worth far more than first place in the swimsuit competition.

"You walked proud, honey," he told me. "I could feel it."

7

Whew! Here I am back at the Holiday Inn, exhausted from the day's emotional intensity. The sesquicentennial celebrations of Fairfield's history are still going on at many locations in town, but the elaborate recognition of the Miss Route 66 Pageant I'd come to sabotage is over. And it was a revelation, I'll tell you, even though things didn't go exactly as I had planned.

I just this minute got off the phone with my husband back in St. Louis, having told him everything that happened. But I know I'm also going to have to write down here what I've confirmed about this town and its past in order to close out a key chapter in my youth . . . and in order to be true to all the girls who competed against each other in a beauty contest so many years ago.

You see, for two decades I've believed that Sally Winchester won the Miss Route 66 crown unfairly. Sure, she looked good in swimsuit and evening gown, and her twirling was dynamite. But she did other things to come out on top, cheating Mary Dunkin, who was first runner-up, and Liz Rogers, who was second runner-up. The rest of us girls were robbed of our chances too, all the way down to the last-place finisher.

I'm not just complaining that Sally did something for Pierce in that changing room backstage that he repaid by talking to the judges. I mean Mayor Rodd, insurance firm owner Mr. Pollman, and lawyer Systrunk all had special reasons to make sure she won. I learned it all that night after the performance, but I didn't think then there was a thing I could do about it.

And I continue to believe that that much, at least, is right: there was nothing that could have been done then. It's taken years of social progress and my own maturing to make possible my confrontation with this ugly phase in Fairfield's history.

My mission today was to tell all, to debunk the pageant's place in Fairfield history (though, of course, it's now the Miss Phipps County Beauty Contest) and to expose the individuals and deeds responsible for the reigns of town beauties over the years.

I'd suggested my place on the program as a "former contestant," not, of course, as a winner. The turnout of past queens was small, and the organizers thought the view of one of the "regular" girls would be nice. My speech, however, was intended to be a shocker.

I was going to tell them what I had concluded after we'd all congratulated Sally and her court: the contest was rigged. Only the naive ones like me had failed to see the clues along the way, the markers of favoritism and influence. We were pawns in a chess game arranged ahead of time by Pierce and certain town officials.

However, before I stepped up to the microphone in the high school auditorium, ready to assert that the pageant had probably been fixed every year, I met Mary at the Dairy Delite (now called Fanny's Route 66 Delite) and we had a good, long talk. It was a talk that forced a change in my plans.

"Sally didn't come?" I asked her, after we'd exchanged the usual hugs, exclamations of pleasure, and summaries of recent events in our respective lives.

"No, she lives in Arizona now, the Phoenix area."

"Shoot! I wanted to see how she'd react to what I'll say."

"What do you mean?"

We were in a booth where I'd often sat with Sandy, though my best friend had, like me, been gone from the Dairy Delite and from Fairfield for years.

"Well, you know," I went on, "Pierce helped her win that crown. And I'm going to do some truth-telling today. Say, where is that old pervert these days anyway?"

It occurred to me I had never heard about Pierce after I graduated from high school. Sure, I repressed thoughts of him whenever I came back for reunions or to visit friends. But he had been pretty well known around town. And I had always assumed he continued to work with Miss Route 66 contestants.

"Oh, long gone. In fact. . . ."

"He should have been run out of town! You know, he propositioned me at the pageant."

"Susan, he propositioned all the girls," she laughed, fingering the mug full of coffee in front of her. "You just turned him down, didn't you?"

"Well, yeah, of course." I'm sure I couldn't conceal the blush I felt rise up from my neck. "But I should have exposed him. He should have been arrested."

"Poor guy, he was all bark and no bite, if you know what I mean. And none of the girls took him up on his offers."

"Oh, Sally did. She must have," I insisted.

"Maybe, but not the way you think."

"What do you mean?"

"Sally actually felt sorry for him. Somehow she knew he wasn't able to function that way. And--not just for that, but for other things, too--his wife was getting ready to leave him. Sally wanted to help him."

"Help him? By fooling around with him?"

"Well, I know it sounds weird. It was certainly weird for those days! But Sally had a kind of a secret. She thought it might, um, excite him."

"You're making this whole thing sound mysterious. Go on."

"Did you know about Sally's car accident? Summer before junior year?"

"I don't remember anything about an accident. She wasn't hurt that badly, was she? I would have heard about it."

232

"A lot of bruises. But the one bad thing was her mouth. Her head crashed into the steering wheel, and . . . well, she lost her teeth."

"All her teeth?" I remembered Blind Bill Martin talking about a funny sound in her speech, a hiss or a slurring. Would that have been caused by false teeth?

Then I thought of something my husband told me after we'd been married a pretty good while, one of those things women of my generation couldn't imagine about men and their lust.

"You mean . . . you mean she told Pierce she had no teeth . . . had false teeth . . . and could . . . gums . . . ?"

"That's right," Mary agreed. "It's some man thing, I guess."

"Gross!"

"Sally knew his wife. Apparently she'd baby-sat their kids when they were much younger. Anyway, she thought just the idea alone might get him, you know, excited. And then. . . ."

"But the pageant was fixed, wasn't it? I mean, Sally's dad was chairman of town council. It was all an inside game: the good old boys who ran Fairfield ran the pageant, and they chose Sally before the competition even began."

"I don't think so, Susan."

"Pierce told me he'd arranged things in other years, knew the judges, picked the winners."

"There was a conspiracy, but it was more a scheme to get Pierce out of the way quietly, not a plan to pick beauty queens."

"What! I don't believe it. How do you know all this?"

"I was the one who finally blew the whistle on Pierce. I told Mr. Blue." He was principal at Fairfield High School.

"When did you do it?"

"About the time our rehearsals for the pageant began. Mr. Pierce came on to me. At first I laughed; then I got mad."

This was a bit embarrassing. He'd tried to seduce me for weeks, but I hadn't done a thing.

"Why didn't they drag him away right then? Charge him with . . . with whatever the charge would be, solicitation of a minor?"

"Susan, you're forgetting how hush-hush anything like this was in those days. Pierce was clever in that way. He knew most girls wouldn't say anything about what he was doing. Some didn't even know what he was asking or hinting at. And, poor guy, he was driven, couldn't help himself."

So the shock of the day came to me, not my audience. Sally Winchester, my most formidable rival, wasn't earning points with the judges by pleasing Pierce. She was some kind of juvenile social worker trying to cure a troubled man! I had not been cheated; the crown had been won fairly and squarely. How wrong about things had I been for so many years? I felt downright dumb.

And then I realized: I had to have a new speech!

8

So, what did I tell the gathering in Fairfield High School's auditorium, those former contestants, judges from the past, fans of beauty contests who turn out year after year? Ooh, I'm embarrassed to admit it! I'll have to confess, but let me at least delay with one digression--a note about Sandy Johnson.

There is one good thing about my performance today, as far as I'm concerned. I didn't have to say what I said to an audience that included Sandy, who would have known how phony I felt I was being in my address to the Miss Route 66 crowd.

I'd corresponded well ahead of time with my best friend growing up, hoping she could be there to offer moral support. After all, she had been my chief fan on the night of the pageant, and she was the first one I had complained to that the contest was a sham. But she was in Europe on a business trip right now and couldn't be here, though she phoned me several times to encourage me in my exposé.

In fact, Sandy, who never entered the Miss Route 66 Pageant, has traveled a lot farther from Fairfield than I did, for all my aspirations that year. Her national and, I suspect, soon-to-be-international experience grew out of her part-time job at Fanny's Dairy Delite.

Mrs. Hamilton and Miss Powers thought Sandy had considerable business sense, and they tried to teach her all they'd learned from setting up and developing an ice cream/sandwich operation.

"It all has to do with traffic," explained Sandy to me one of those vacations when I was back from college. She had gone a year to South Central Missouri State in town, one of the few girls to attend there. All those months, though, she continued to work part time at Fanny's. Then she dropped out of school completely to concentrate on expanding their operation.

"Traffic?" I wondered.

"Sure. You have to be where the customers will be. Think of Fanny's. It's on Route 66, see? A major east-west route, so plenty of out-of-state travelers have come by here."

"Yeah. That makes sense."

"Not only that, local people have a tendency to do their around-town trips along such a thoroughfare."

"OK, I believe you. But I'm not so sure on that one."

I didn't think of myself as a local girl any more, by the way. After my second year at Northeast Missouri State, I worked in St. Louis over the summers and kept my visits to family brief. I felt I'd never come back to live in Fairfield with its provincial mores and commitment to the status quo.

"I watched my classmates," Sandy continued, "those who stayed on in town. They didn't want to leave the familiar, their friends and family. But even people who've lived here forever like thinking about the possibility of change. And they know how roads in town connect up to state and national roads. So they tend to go out of their way to end up driving those bigger routes."

"Hmm."

"So, Fanny's has always been in a good spot. Not a perfect spot, though."

"How so?"

"Well, when they built the bypass--and later the Interstate--no place had the same advantage of being in town and along a national highway at the same time. You were either in town or along the highway, except for those out-of-town folks who come into town to get gas or eat or something."

"Fanny's still going strong, though," I noted.

"It is, but not as strong as it might be."

"You have a strategy for that?"

"I do," said Sandy. It turned out, she had a strategy that would be far more successful than anyone had anticipated.

As the two older ladies' heiress apparent at Fanny's, Sandy had implemented a program that sustained the operation through changing times and prepared the way for her own later business venture. The key to her plan was the symbol.

Once the major highways had bypassed in-town establishments, Sandy reasoned, local people couldn't feel they were on nation-crossing paths during their daily driving. They would have to go out of town--say, to Jefferson City or St. Louis--to capture that connection to grander destinies. But they might feel connected if an establishment like Fanny's Dairy Delite emphasized its place on larger maps through symbolic representation.

So Sandy changed the name of Mrs. Hamilton's and Miss Powers' place to Fanny's Route 66 Delite and began decorating the place with icons of the highway and its glorious past. She found and framed old magazine photos of cars and gas stations. She collected memorabilia from the Depression and the World War II era, especially roadside attractions like Burma Shave signs and "See Meramec Cavern" posters.

She gave Fanny's a new theme, that is, and her timing was perfect. As America moved on in the turbulent 1960s, as two-lane roads gave way to limited-access superhighways, people wanted to retain a sense that they belonged, even if it was to an older order. Against the hurry and unsettled nature of the present, Sandy provided a nostalgic atmosphere of the good old days.

The strategy worked so well Sandy later opened her own business--not a "Mom and Pop" operation, but a "Mom" one. Out on the western edge of town, where the business route connected with Interstate 44 (the highway that replaced old Route 66), she built her first Mom's Business Cafe.

She catered to through drivers, who could see her advertising along the roadway, and to town folk, who were reached by word of mouth. Mom's did so well, Sandy soon had restaurants across the state, then across the Midwest, and now she's going national.

Each Mom's re-creates the homey atmosphere of a family restaurant in a distinctly feminine mode, but it's run with the efficiency believed to characterize a masculine business approach. Decor and menu draw on both realms. Perhaps as important to success has been her choice of location--places that feel both local and connected by routes that go on to distant, well-known destinations.

So Sandy analyzed the traffic and positioned herself to profit from it. I, on the other hand, have been settled in St. Louis for several decades, building a stable family and playing the flute. I'll tell you more about my music career in just a minute, as all the pieces of my story seem to be coming together here. Not in the way I had imagined, but perhaps in a satisfying pattern nonetheless.

But here first are the key elements of the speech I delivered to all those Fairfieldians still interested in Miss Route 66.

I couldn't, of course, go ahead with my declaration that the whole thing had been a sham, that winners were picked ahead of time by a close circle of old men. Mary had disabused me of that notion. But there I was on the program, committed to speaking as one of the hundreds of girls whose lives had been improved by participation in the process.

And that's, in fact, pretty much what I ended up saying! I began with my impulsive purchase of a flute, saying that becoming a contestant must have been in the back of my mind all the time. I'd just needed a reason to explore my own potential for music, for a public life.

The weeks of practice on my own and then during the final days of rehearsal were important steps in my development. And not just as flutist or as model for swimsuit or evening gown, but as young person emerging into adulthood. Even though school and church were working toward the same ends, the Miss Route 66 contest had given me an extra measure of self-confidence that had generated benefits for me ever since.

Then I had to say that working with the other girls had not been a dog-eat-dog competition, but an effort in cooperation, shared experience, bonding with those who were trying for the same prize. When we teared up as Sally stepped forward to show her crown, it was not with jealousy or regret but with joy at her success.

I mean to tell you, I laid it on, giving the citizens of Fairfield just what they wanted to hear. And the thing is, by the time I was done, I found I believed it myself!

9

Oh, well, not every bit of it.

There are, I know, better ways to develop feminine self-confidence than through beauty contests. And as we've come to provide other avenues, we've moved forward as a society.

Too, there's something fundamentally flawed about this subject-object relationship endorsed by a beauty contest in which men judge women. Women are subjects also, you know, thinking beings who look at the world even as the world looks at them.

But, for me, the pageant began or continued some important changes in how I'd thought of myself, of what I wanted do with the rest of my life. I think I've always known that, even if I believed the thing had been rigged.

Mary's explanation of the real plot--to get Pierce out of the way quietly--makes a fair amount of sense, though. She said that hers had not been the first complaint about the assistant principal. But while people like Mayor Rodd had at first dismissed such suspicions, Mary's testimony changed their mind.

Her father, Marvin Dunkin, had also spoken to a lawyer, who'd talked with the chief of police. So it was decided that, in order to avoid embarrassment for the town, Pierce would be allowed to complete the current pageant. But he would lose his job as assistant principal after he admitted to unnamed "errors in judgment" in the carrying out of his duties. It was not a severe punishment, but it forced him out of education.

The other key witness to the solicitations was Blind Bill Martin. He'd overheard enough of what Pierce said to me and, on other occasions, to Sally to convince any last skeptics among the powers that be.

Not knowing all this, though, I was mad at everyone that night. And for days afterwards I kept thinking that Pierce had not been alone in a cruel effort to take advantage of Fairfield girls. But I didn't tell anyone except Sandy and--by complete accident--Larry Thornton. And I wouldn't have told him either if I hadn't gotten flustered in the family bomb shelter.

You see, we had that date I'd agreed to shortly after the pageant. He became the first boy to take me out to dinner. We went to a family-style restaurant on old Business Route 66 at the west edge of town. He was a lot more restrained on this date than Randy had ever been, and he surprised the heck out of me when he suggested we come back to my house, watch TV with my parents or just chat. This pleased Mom and Dad enormously.

"Larry, what are you going to do with your life?" asked my dad. He was surprisingly animated for a Friday evening, even turning down the volume on the TV so we could all talk.

"I'm going to be a lawyer, sir."

"Ah, the law. Yes."

"I thought you would stay in science, Larry," I said. "After all your science fair projects, especially those worms."

"The two things might be related," he explained.

"What do you mean, Larry?" asked my mother. She was bringing a tray of cookies from the kitchen.

"Everyone needs representation," said Larry, taking a cookie and a paper napkin. "Even animals sometimes."

"You're going to be a worm lawyer?" I couldn't help asking, though I said it with a smile, amused but not as if I disapproved.

"Probably not a worm lawyer," he chuckled. "But I might represent those farmers who care about the animals they raise. They don't always get the breaks when competing with other farmers. The small farmer has it especially hard, battling those guys that own lots of land and raise huge herds of livestock."

"I think worms need representation," offered my dad, turning down the cookies Mom held poised before him. He'd actually lost a few pounds recently, trimming his pear-shaped middle enough for the women in his family to notice.

"Oh? Worms?" wondered my mother.

"You see, Larry," continued my dad, leaning toward my date as if the two were working closely together. "Years ago, I built a bomb shelter, set into the bank on the property here."

"I've heard about that, sir. It's supposed to be quite sophisticated."

"It is. And it's made me think about creatures that live underground, that know the earth from the inside, so to speak."

"Worms live in the dark," agreed Larry. "And they're always at work in there, transforming waste material into foodstuff for others in the animal and plant kingdoms."

"Yes, that's what I mean. Out of sight, quiet, but doing good. They should have lawyers!" he concluded with a laugh.

"I'd like to see that bomb shelter of yours sometime," said Larry. And I knew we were in for it.

"No time like the present," said my dad, popping up. "Grab your coat and follow me. You too, Susan."

"I think I've seen it, Dad."

But he wasn't to be denied. And I knew I had to stick with my date this evening. Mom was able to claim cleanup duties in the kitchen.

Dad gave an informed tour, providing explanations of both the shelter's features and its construction. Larry ooh-ed and ahh-ed as any boy should in the presence of his date's father's creation.

"Water stored here," said Dad, pointing to U.S. Army surplus containers.

"Ah, handy to the sink and the stove."

"Kerosene lamps here where you won't bump into them when the power goes." They were set neatly in little nooks in the wall.

"Ooh, that's good thinking."

I must have stopped paying very careful attention to this dialogue of mutual enthusiasm and began poking around in the books and magazines put away for reading in the days of Apocalypse. Neville Shute's *On the Beach* probably couldn't have been in my hands then, but somehow that's how I remember the scene.

Then I became aware of Larry's saying, "You seemed pretty upset that night at the pageant."

"I . . . uh. . . ." I looked around. Dad had left. The two of us were alone in the main room of the shelter, a dim light softening the look of everything. I don't know that there was romantic music, but in my memory Dad has left a radio on.

"Sally's hard to beat," Larry offered.

He'd told me this several times already, and I was ready to shrug, to move on to another topic.

"You were cheated," Larry concluded.

"I know it!" I burst out. "That Pierce, and the others, they got together."

Larry hadn't meant this literally, however. He just meant that I didn't get the scores I deserved, that the judges didn't make good evaluations.

"Oh, I don't know about that," he continued, a look of sudden alarm on his face.

"I'm telling you they cheated me. And . . . and the other girls too. Sally, she did favors for the judges, like, kissed them and stuff."

"What!"

246

"I'm not going to talk about it. But it's unfair. I wouldn't do that thing Pierce wanted, you know. . . ."

"You were asked to . . . um. . . ." Larry couldn't put this into words either. We young people didn't have a ready public vocabulary for such an exchange in those days. But he seemed to understand enough to get mad, to get red in the face, to puff and to blow. "That's . . . I . . . you. . . ."

"I thought about challenging the results, pointing a finger at those guys. But I was all alone."

"Let me represent you," he said.

"What? Be my lawyer?" I laughed. He sounded so formal, so serious. "You're just starting college next fall, not law school!"

"Let me represent you," he said again with a funny smile.

"I'm all right. I'm not going to sue or anything. You don't need to represent me."

"No," Larry said. And, suddenly, he put his arms around me. I started, but didn't pull away. "I mean," he concluded. "I mean, marry me."

10

Did I accept Larry's proposal? Well, of course not, at least not on the night of our first date out in the Bell family bomb shelter. But I did say yes to his request for a second date. And we were a couple through the rest of our senior year.

A lot was happening then, changes in me and changes in my family. So, I wasn't ready to make any big decision about my life so quickly after the Miss Route 66 Pageant.

Perhaps the least-changing figure near the center of my world was my older sister, Tricia. She remained on her course to stardom, standing out at Drury and landing a part in a summer theatrical group that toured the Midwest. We'd always felt she was destined to shine, and these accomplishments maintained that predictable trajectory.

Tricia did not let her success overshadow my small triumph in competing in the local pageant, however. In all our family discussions she insisted I should have been one of the finalists.

"And no matter what," she told me at dinner the next night. "You have to keep up your music. I only wish I could play the way you do!"

She had asked that afternoon to hear me play everything in my repertoire, apologizing repeatedly for not having noticed in earlier visits how quickly I had acquired this skill.

"Mom's the one you should listen to, though," I insisted. Mom joined me on a few duets, but reluctantly. I guess she, too, felt it was my time to get the attention.

"Oh, I know she's good," Tricia went on. "Did she tell you about the orchestra?"

"What orchestra? No. Mom?"

"Oh, it's a little thing, and it may not even happen. I also didn't want to distract you the last few weeks as this project was taking shape. You had your own important things to see to."

"Tell me," I insisted.

"Oh, you know Madeline Powers, at the Dairy Delite?"

"Sure. She's one of Sandy's bosses. Nice lady."

"Well, she's also the leader of a group trying to start up a municipal orchestra. A small one, of course. But they would like me to play with them."

"What a neat idea!" I said. But I was still surprised that I'd heard nothing about this before.

"Yes, Mayor Rodd's been very enthusiastic. We think he can persuade the town council to give us a little help financially."

My enthusiasm for the project lessened with this announcement, since I believed the mayor to be part of the plot that had kept me from being Miss Route 66. But Mom showed no apprehension about working with any town official or corporate sponsor. And I'm glad to think now that any worry I might have had about her vulnerability was unjustified.

Now that I think back about it, I remember that Mr. Systrunk also helped in the early days of the Fairfield City Orchestra, finding a temporary practice space for the group in the old shoe factory building on 7th Street, which had stood empty for a number of years.

But Mom stayed with this fledgling musical group until she and Dad retired to Arizona, performing a series of concerts each year in Fairfield and occasionally traveling to smaller towns in the area for additional appearances. Other parents began asking her to teach their children, and she gave lessons at our home all the years I was away at college and then while my children were growing up.

A new pastime took shape in my father's life at the same time as he became an avid golfer. It began as a way to get in shape (which worked), but he kept on playing when he realized he was pretty good at it.

As his pear-shaped belly got slimmer, his drives went longer and his putts more true. The college golf course offered reasonable rates to locals, and their added fees helped fund improvements. So he played there twice a week except during the hard winter and was a regular in area tournaments.

As I approach the date of my own children's' going off to college, I see that my parents dealt with their empty nest pretty well. New activities, new horizons for them both. But since music and golf had been part of their lives at earlier times, a return to them also gave a certain completeness to their stories.

250

As I've said, I came home infrequently during the next few years. I was asserting my independence. And Tricia was moving in steady steps toward Broadway and her acting success. So we sisters generally saw this resumption of our mother's music career and our father's golf playing primarily as background to our own concerns.

Juliet, the parrot I'd kept that fall, went back to Springfield with Tricia right after the pageant. A mate from Africa was waiting for Juliet at Tricia's friend's apartment near campus, and, last I heard, those two feathered creatures were still together, lovers for life.

"Hello there. Come here," said Juliet when I was packing up her food and all her little toys.

"Yeah, I know, I know," I agreed. "'Pretty bird.'"

"She's a talker, isn't she," said my sister, putting a finger up to the cage for Juliet to rub against and pull on with her hooked beak.

"Say, Tricia, I never did ask you, who taught this bird to speak?"

"You mean, the 'pet me' part?" she said with a giggle.

"I . . . uh . . . well, yes, all her words." I was embarrassed. Did she understand how "pet me" had inspired me to explore my own capacity for pleasure?

Tricia gave me a little hug. "Little sister," she said. "I think it might be, it could just be, it probably was . . . me."

She detached Juliet's cage from its stand and tripped downstairs, humming a little tune. Had she meant what I thought she meant here? I didn't know, and didn't know how to pursue it.

Well, who understands, anyway, where ideas come from, what the wells of inspiration are that we tap in trying new things. Life is a series of unknowns we take on with fear and trepidation.

How do we find what it takes to make it through challenging situations, me at the Miss Route 66 Pageant, for instance? We hope for new skills to meet the unfamiliar. And we count on strengths gained in previous struggles.

Of course, all my family helped me that year. And Larry.

Larry still helps.

I did, you see, marry him in the summer before our senior year of college. We'd been unhappy waiting for letters to travel to and from Columbia and Springfield (I was not at Drury, but Southeast Missouri State).

The declaration of our intention that June was the most shocking announcement I ever made to my parents, more shocking even than my revelation that the flute on the dining room table was mine. I'd expected an explosion, especially from my dad, since we'd all assumed we could wait until graduation. But after the initial surprise, they took it pretty much in stride. Parents do that more often than they get credit for.

"He's a fine boy," my father said. "You two have been mighty unhappy apart."

"And we'll both finish college, just not in the same year." I'd insisted Larry stay in school while I worked the next year, then we'd change roles for me to graduate. It wasn't ideal, but Washington University later let him delay his entrance to law school for those two semesters and we didn't feel we'd lost anything. I wasn't going to live away from the man I love, and I haven't ever again. I'll be in his arms tonight after the drive up I-44 to our home in Chesterfield.

We don't raise worms, but daughters, fine daughters who have no particular desire to win beauty contests. They'd rather be successful lawyers like their dad.

Still, they both play music like their mother and grandmother. I guess "Do-re-mi-fa-sol-la-ti-do" runs in the family. And they enjoy the story we all tell about how I once, almost, very nearly was Fairfield's own Miss Route 66.

The End

Epilogue

What ever happened to Mr. Pierce? It's the last thing I'll write, an unhappy postscript to my own happy life history. Well, my life history to this point, I guess I should say.

I heard the last chapter of Pierce's story just yesterday, one year after my dramatic return to Fairfield and my anticlimactic speech to the gathering of Miss Route 66 Pageant fans. My husband gave me the news.

Larry was on the edge of our bed sipping a glass of Perrier while I considered what to wear to a fund raiser for the junior symphony, in which our daughters have played. He already had on one of his dark suits. I was in bare feet and a slip.

"They're fixing up the airport, did I tell you?" Larry said.

"They're always working on it. Nice?" I had hung two outfits in front of the walk-in closet in our bedroom.

"Actually, yes, though some parts aren't finished."

I stepped up to one outfit, adjusted the shoulder on the hanger, stepped back to look again. It resembled slightly, I realized, the evening gown I'd worn so many years ago in the Miss Route 66 competition.

"There's a whole new lounge where I waited for our client to come in."

"Do you like the blue or the gray?" I asked.

"Gray. There's a new men's room in the concourse where I was, new but strange."

"Gray? Do I have the right shoes?" I rummaged around on the floor of the closet.

"It's wonderful to find an absolutely clean men's room. Maybe I was their very first customer, using the only clean urinal in America. White, vestal, virgin."

"You don't like the blue?" I looked at it again, taking a step back, considering. I thought for a moment how I'd look at the fund raiser, what sort of figure I'd present to fellow supporters of the arts.

"Uh, yes." I seemed to have thrown him off a minute. "I do like the blue. I like them both."

"You like them both?" I reached past them into the closet to pull out a third set, a white blouse with flowery skirt--deep colors--and red sash, which I carried over to the full-length mirror on the back of the door.

"So, in the new men's room at the airport," Larry went on, recalling his story. He took a sip of water. "I did what I'd come for, stepped back to flush and couldn't find a handle, or a button, or a pedal."

"Don't tell me they forgot?" I was looking at the three choices, chuckling to myself at the thought of the evening's being a beauty contest, a showing of women and men.

"No, at least I don't think so. Anyway, I gave up looking after a minute, went around to the other side, where the sinks were, and, just as I turned the corner, I heard a flush."

"The whole row?"

"No. Just mine."

"Must be on some sort of timer. Automatic, serial."

"Or, probably," he said, "it's some photoelectric device, five seconds after you break the plane, whoosh."

"Hmm," I said. He was wondering, I figured, how he looked in that row of men at that row of urinals.

"But then, I thought, perhaps size is a factor. I stepped back in front and pretended. Maybe there's a minimum. You know, to trigger things. It's a new measure of America, that's it!" He was getting into it now, up off the bed pacing, eyeing me for a response. Now I suspected there was more to this little story than I'd thought at first.

"Can you see those dark-suited businessmen, commuting to New York for a day's meeting, wondering, 'Am I all right? Did I trigger that thing or was it the guy next to me?' Think of how adolescent boys would feel, intimidated. How about football teams on a road trip, what a show!"

"Oh me," I said. I turned to face him, my three shadow selves arranged behind me. He took a ball point pen from his pocket and rang the glass with it. Ding-ding-ding!

"But, of course, you don't have to worry," he said, pointing. "On my second try, not only did my urinal fire, but the ones on each side! Whoosh, whoosh, whoosh." He was coming up to me. "Shoot, I had to get out of there, the whole wall was starting to shake, know what I mean? They were all flushing."

I was smiling now too, because I knew what he was doing. Oh, men! You poor sad creatures, pulled around by desire. He dipped his finger into the glass of water he was holding.

"One of the units was about to overflow and rolls of toilet paper were popping out of stalls, coming across the floor, and . . . and. . . ." He waved wildly. "Two of the hot air dryers cut on and the doors swung open. I think there was music. Yes, a powerful, erotic hum! Rrrruummm!" He placed his wet fingertip on the lip of the glass and dragged it around the edge.

I held up the blue outfit on its hanger, a shield against this sex maniac. He set the glass on the dresser, put his arms around me, and tried to back me toward the bed.

"We have to get ready. Stop that!" I said, but he was funny.

"Stop? A real man can't stop."

"He can if he's married and over forty-five and has to be across town in thirty minutes."

"No, no!"

"And if he gets a promise about later. . . ."

That stopped him. "Later? You're sure."

Then, his face changed, went sober all of a sudden.

258

"What?" I asked, giving him a light kiss.

"I'd repressed telling you, but . . . but that . . " He pointed to the glass resting on the dresser top. "It reminded me. I heard about old Mr. Pierce this week."

"The Senior Consultant to the Miss Route 66 Pageant, the Fairfield High School assistant principal? I've always wondered what happened to him."

I took the gray outfit off its hanger, stepped into the skirt, and went over in front of the mirror.

"Well, Pierce is dead. Suicide. Happened more than fifteen years ago. The new guy in our office, he grew up in Neosho. That's where Pierce went after Fairfield."

"I'm sorry. That's sad."

"It is. The story was he never could control himself, his, um, urges. There was another incident with a young girl and . . . well. . . . He knew he was headed for prison this time."

Larry stood behind me for a minute, his arms around my waist. Then he said, "I'll wait for you downstairs."

Larry knows that the minutes wives spend every day in front of a mirror are not simply time devoted to examining or adjusting what we look like. The fluffing of hair, the arched neck to achieve different views, the steps back for inspection are really parts of a deliberate composition of the self. Right then I needed a little extra time to compose myself.

When I examine myself, I often think of my mother and all the times I came looking for help with school projects, music lessons, boyfriend questions. She was in front of her mirror drawing upon deep inner strength unavailable to so many people. Our daughters have inherited the practice, studying, not themselves in the mirror, but possibilities. "Do-re-mi-fa-sol-la-ti-do," we all hum, seeing deeper than faces, bodies, poses.

That's probably why I turned against beauty pageants in general along with many in my generation. They're by definition superficial. Judges rank the outer you, no matter how much time is given to talent, questions-and-answers on world issues, personal accomplishments.

This doesn't mean I don't want men to look at me, especially Larry, who also wants me to look at him. When we come back from the fund raiser, I'll give his only slightly pear-shaped belly a score. And he can appreciate my flat tummy, which he never fails to do. But we see so much more in each other that what's outside is made beautiful no matter its flaws.

I'm not Miss Route 66, you know. But I do wear proudly the crown of Susan Bell Thornton.

Route 66 books by Michael Lund

Growing Up on Route 66 — Michael Lund (2000) ISBN 1-888725-31-1 Novel evoking fond memories of what it was like to grow up alongside "America's Highway" in 20th Century Missouri. (Trade paperback) 5x8 260 pp,

Route 66 Kids — Michael Lund (2002) ISBN 1-888725-70-2 Sequel to *Growing Up on Route 66*, continuing memories of what it was like to grow up alongside "America's Highway" in 20th Century Missouri. (Trade paperback) 5x8 270 pp,

A Left-hander on Route 66--Michael Lund (2003) ISBN 1-888725-88-5. Twenty years after the fact, left-hander Hugh Noone appeals a wrongful conviction that detoured him from "America's Main Street" and put him in jail. But revealing the details of the past and effecting a resolution of his case mean a dramatic rearrangement of his world, including troubled relationships with three women: Linda Roy, Patty Simpson, and Karen Murphy. (Trade paperback) 5x8 270 pp

Route 66 Spring-- Michael Lund (2004) ISBN: 1-888725-98-2. The lives of four young Missourians are changed when a bottle comes to the surface of one of the state's many natural springs. Inside is a letter written by a girl a dozen years after the end of the Civil War. Lucy Rivers Johns ' epistle contains a sad story of family failure and a powerful plea for help. This message from the last century crystallizes the individual frustrations of Janet Masters, Freddy Sills, Louis Clark, and Roberta Green, another group of Route 66 kids. Their response to the past charts a bold path into the future, a path inspired by the Mother Road itself. (Trade paperback) 5x8 270 pp,

Miss Route 66--Michael Lund (2004) ISBN 1-888725-96-6. In the fourth novel of Michael Lund's Route 66 Novel Series, Susan Bell tells the story of her candidacy in Fairfield, Missouri's annual beauty contest. Now married and with teenage children in St. Louis, she recounts her youthful adventure in this small town along "America's Highway." At the same time, she plans a return to Fairfield in order to right injustices she feels were done to some young contestants in the Miss Route 66 Pageant. (Trade paperback) 5½ X8¼, 260 pp **Audiobook** on 5 CD's ISBN 1-888725-12-5

Route 66 to Vietnam Michael Lund (2004) ISBN 1-59630-000-0 This novel takes characters from earlier works in the Route 66 Novel Series farther west than Los Angeles, official destination of the famous highway, Route 66. Mark Landon and Billy Rhodes find the values they grew up on challenged by America's role in Southeast Asia. But elements of their upbringing represented by the Mother Road also sustain them in ways they could never have anticipated. . (Trade paperback) 5½ X8¼, 270 pp,

AudioBook on CD—Route 66 to Vietnam ISBN: 1-59630-011-6 Michael Lund's fictional commentary from the viewpoint of a draftee. by Michael Lund unabridged 6 CD's --9 hours running time.

Route 66 Chapel Michael Lund (2006) ISBN 1-59630-012-4 Route 66 Chapel, Michael Lund (2006)

(Trade paperback) 5½ X8¼, 260 pp,. When the
forces of progress threaten the foundation of
smalltown life — a small church — five senior citizens,
a mysterious newcomer, and one young couple band
together in an unlikely campaign to save it. The
embattled meeting point of old and new is Route 66
Chapel, a building curiously linked to America's
"Mother Road."

Route 66 Choir-- A Comedy (2010)

Michael Lund ISBN 9781596300583   284 pp 5" x 8"
In Route 66 Choir Stanley Measure takes
early retirement just before September 11, 2001, and
his impulsive decisions participate in an unraveling
of confidence in the American way of life. His wife
Felicia finds that everything she holds dear is in
danger of coming apart: her marriage, her church,
her business, and even her country. Who or what can
orchestrate the recovery of harmony necessary to
sustain the spirit of the Mother Road?

Route 66 Bride (Fall 2010)

BeachHouse
Books

www.beachhousebooks.com

an Imprint of
Science & Humanities Press
PO Box 7151
Chesterfield, MO 63006-
7151
(636) 394-4950

Our books are guaranteed:

If a book has a defect, or doesn't hold up under normal use, or if you are unhappy in any way with one of our books, we are interested to know about it and will replace it and credit reasonable return shipping costs. Products with publisher defects (i.e., books with missing pages, etc.) may be returned at any time without authorization. However, we request that you describe the problem, to help us to continuously improve.

Educators Discount Policy

To encourage use of our books for education, educators can purchase three or more books (mixed titles) on our standard discount schedule for resellers. See **sciencehumanitiespress.com/educator/educator.htm** l for more detail or call Science & Humanities Press, PO Box 7151, Chesterfield MO 63006-7151636-394-4950

www.ingramcontent.com/pod-product-compliance
Lightning Source LLC
Chambersburg PA
CBHW071127260626
47162CB00003B/690